DROP ME OFF IN HARLEM

A Murder Mystery

By Sondra Luger

Gotham Books

30 N Gould St.
Ste. 20820, Sheridan, WY 82801
https://gothambooksinc.com/
Phone: 1 (307) 464-7800

© 2022 Sondra Luger. All rights reserved.

No part of this book may be reproduced, stored in a retrieval system, or transmitted by any means without the written permission of the author.

Published by Gotham Books (July 14, 2022)

ISBN: 979-8-88775-004-0 (sc)
ISBN: 979-8-88775-005-7 (e)

This is a work of fiction. Names, characters, places, and incidents are either the product of the author's imagination or are used fictitiously, and a resemblance to actual persons, living or dead, business establishments, any events or locales is entirely coincidental.

Because of the dynamic nature of the Internet, any web addresses or links contained in this book may have changed since publication and may no longer be valid. The views expressed in this work are solely those of the author and do not necessarily reflect the views of the publisher, and the publisher hereby disclaims any responsibility for them.

GOTHAM BOOKS

DEDICATION

In Memory Of

Lillian Rosen Luger

High Fashion Model

Drop Me Off In Harlem

CHAPTER ONE

The tip of her hat was jauntily in the air, defiant almost, but Lily was not the defiant type, though no female would blame her if she were. How dare Walter Martin fire her when she kept the office books so neatly, was so polite and deferential, despite his grunting and his bullying of son Ted. So what if the young man helped her during his lunch hour, drove her home and picked her up each morning? They weren't engaged, for goodness's sake, nor had they any intention of being-well, she had no intention of being. Marriage was out of the question for now. An opera career came first. Well, actually, earning enough money for more lessons came first, and she had started late. Twenty-four was practically senile for a beginner. She sighed. At least Monster Martin had given her five recommendations to businesses he supplied with fabric. And maybe not so monster, either. Ted's attentions, while flattering, weren't really welcome. He'd given hints --- housewife, tending three kids, maybe a housemaid, if his father gave him a raise. Poor deluded Ted. What century was he living in? It was 1927; the shackles were off; skirts were at the knees --- yes, Monster Martin, at the knees and her hair was almost as short as Ted's. She walked up the stairs to number five on her list. Number four had wanted an experienced model, number three had wanted someone trained by John Robert Powers, number two had wanted someone trained, experienced, and "familiar" with the buyers, and number one had wanted someone who had worked for Patou. Lily looked up at the towering wooden doors. Short hair, short skirts and tall buildings, she mused. Amazing, but opposites, seem to have an affinity for each other. She paused for a moment inside the massive lobby before striding across the black and white tiled floor to the imposing mahogany desk.

"Singer Couture?"

"Second floor. Elevator on your left, ma'am."

Serious faces all, she thought, as she entered the box. Sharp nose, straight-brimmed hat. An accountant? Slicked hair, bow tie. An attorney? Small brimmed hat, long skirt, square jacket, brown paper bag. A secretary? No one smiled, no one talked, no one moved. Second floor. All Singer Couture. A nickel toss. She walked to the right down a long, narrow corridor until ah, yes! She opened the glass block door. The receptionist's desk was low and uncluttered. A chignoned Miss Prim sat behind it.

"Yes?"

"I hope that will be Mr. Singer's answer," responded Lily, as she handed Monster's recommendation to the unsmiling, spectacled woman behind the barricade.

"Too late," she said. "We had a position, but it has been filled."

"That letter was for Mr. Singer." Lily's eyes darkened.

"I am the business manager. I speak for Mr. Singer. Good day." "I'm sorry, but I must see Mr. Singer himself. And it won't be a good day to me if I don't get a job."

"That's not our affair, young lady. I'm sorry, truly I am," she said without passion. "Good day." Her voice escalated to override music emanating from nearby.

A portly gentleman emerged from a corridor to the left of the desk. "Margaret, call me immediately when our soprano arrives.

Francois insists the rehearsal must include her." And he disappeared down the corridor. Lily had turned. She hesitated at the door. Then, swinging her reticule four times, as she did when she was excited, she emitted a curdling high C. Margaret's mouth flew open in shock and terror, and Lily flew down the corridor after her quarry.

His head shot out of a doorway. "Miss Revilier? It's about time!" And he hastily ushered her in.

Margaret Snotnose marched down the corridor, knocked on a door beyond which peals of masculine laughter could be heard, and entered without awaiting a response.

"Miss Revilier, your soprano, has arrived."

"She certainly has," responded Bernard Singer, smiling broadly, "and her name is Lily Ann Chasen. Put her on the books at $60 a week."

"One week at $60," she uttered primly.

"No, Margaret, $60 in perpetuity, subject to raises, of course," he turned to explain to Lily.

"As what?" Prim demanded.

"Model," he replied. "And singer, and do you sketch?"

"Yes," Lily ad-libbed. How hard could it be to learn?

"And sketcher, and whatever."

"Whatever?" she repeated, aghast, and made a hurried exit before she was subjected to hearing more.

Chapter Two

Lily Chasen was not interested in fashion, well, not fashion as such. If it made her more comfortable, met a practical need, then yes, she was interested. So she was interested in keeping her hair short and hiding it under a cloche with merely peek-a-boo waves protruding from the sides, and she was interested in shorter dresses, which allowed her freer movement, and if the limp frock accentuated the underweight body so in vogue now, all the better. She could be both comfortable and "in." Bustles and bones had contorted the body in an era of buxom bliss. That era was gone. Looking good made her feel good for herself, not for a man. The world had gone faddish, maddish. She longed to enter an opera era of long ago that reflected the best, most practical elements of today. Fat chance of that!

So, here she was, a stranger again in the city of her birth, in the Garment District, instead of The Manhattan School of Music, in the superficial quiet of frantic Singer Couture. "You're on next, you're on next, you're on next!" Thank you, Ginger, Sally and Margo. After a month she knew enough to know when she was on, unlike her one-year stint at Walter Martin Fabrics. But dear Ted had kindly known when she was "on," when deliveries were due, pickups scheduled and invoices mailed out. Here she was on her own, with an audience to fuel an angry Bernard Singer if she was not "on." Francois had just finished singing Margo's frock onto the runway, and now, sheet music in hand, she would do the same for hers, a Singer innovation that pleased the ladies sipping tea or coffee and munching buttered biscuits at the round, cozy, "personal" tables, as Bernard Singer called them. She strolled, paused and hurried back to the dressing room for the next garment. She quickly picked up the clothes that had been dropped on the floor, Singer's reprimand, "You're here to model, not pick up after the other girls!" still ringing in her ears. She put a stunning coat over her dress to make her next entrance in the weekly Singer Collection show. Lily fingered the broad sweep of fur swirling around the neck of her collar and down the front of the coat. Bernard Singer had softened the rabbit so that it almost felt like mink, and he had edged it in lamb, the kind of miracle and added grace he was known for in the trade. From Paris with the Singer touch. Lily appreciated her good fortune --- wearing, at least briefly, beautiful clothes in a fashion house models would die to work for. She was not sure she would have gained ready entrée had Singer's latest creative idea not required a soprano to steep his clothes in a romantic aura women would admire. She was relaxed as she approached the microphone. Tenisha Jones, alert, but never looking relaxed, was ready, list in hand, to retrieve special requests after the presentation ended, which it soon would. Sue's fingers touched the piano's keys as her head nodded the downbeat, and Lily, an octave lower than she would have liked, began: "The fur is cozy, warm and chic, the edge of lamb divine. A bit more leg and oh, the waist is mine!" Having prepared the ladies for this wonder, she stepped onto the stage, walked its length and back, then down the six stairs, slowly, smilingly moving in circular fashion around the tables, pausing for a patron's touch or admiration, while Sue played a romantic staple and a season's hit. Then, she was out a side door and back to the dressing room for her next garment in the show, a woolen wonder with a pinched waist.

Lizette was pinning a flower to the bosom of the dress she would soon model. "Good, good," she said, pointing to the speaker above the door. "But I tell you again to sing in French. Before Patou I sang, and got compliments for the clothes."

"Maybe for the clothes, but the ladies won't understand."

"Not important to understand, only to feel. The French way. Do they understand Francois? They feel his words."

Lily had, in fact, just begun French lessons, and the beginner's book was tucked in her reticule reposing in the locked closet. But telling Lizette, or showing her the profusely illustrated volume, might only bring laughter. The French model, who had spent two years at Patou, laughed a lot and had not, as yet, endeared herself to the Singer mannequins.

"Maybe French --- soon," Lily allowed herself to say.

"Foolish to wait," said Lizette, as she began to exit the dressing room. She paused. "Are you busy later, Lee?"

"Why, no."

"Good."

Lily sighed. Too bad Singer didn't want French opera sung to his patrons. She'd learn the language very fast for that! She grabbed some lyrics and slowly walked backstage humming. She saw a stony-faced Lizette heading back to the dressing room. "Sheesh, what a stiff!" said Maryanne, as she adjusted her dress collar. "Oh, I don't know," said Lily, still amazed that Lizette could be so warm to her and so cool to the other models.

The pinched waist was a hit. It wouldn't have been, thought Lily, without Madam Rosenthal's Maiden Form brassiere. She wondered which was more daring, flapper flat or hint of bosom. "Depends on occasion, age and object to impress," Lizette had told her, but bosom was Lizette's overwhelming favorite when she left Singer Couture for "the real world." For her real world, anyway, whatever that is, thought Lily. She went backstage for her final song for Singer's take on a Chanel blouse. Francois waited patiently to sing his kinswoman onstage.

Bernard Singer, agitated, approached Lily. "Lee, when you're finished, get Lizette."

"She'll be here any minute. You know she's never late."

Five minutes later, Lily hurried to the dressing room, as a nervous Singer paced backstage. The room seemed empty. Then, with a sharp intake of breath, she hurried to the woman on the floor and knelt beside her. A quick check made it clear that Lizette was beyond help. Suddenly, the door opened. Tenisha Jones, her smooth black skin now pale in shock and horror, stood in the doorway. Lily pulled off her dress and struggled to remove Lizette's. "Help me!" she begged, but the business manager's assistant stood frozen in place. At last Lily succeeded, and pulled her colleague's dress over her own head, adjusting it as she ran to the door.

"Take care of this!" she hurled, as she passed Tenisha. "She's yours now, Lord," Lily mumbled as she dashed for the stage.

"Have mercy!"

CHAPTER THREE

"Miss Chasen, you're first because you happened to find the body."

Lily stared at Detective Inspector Kirk. "She was late to the stage."

"You stripped off her dress, put it on and dashed to substitute. Signs of someone swift, efficient, practical."

One out of three right isn't bad, thought Lily. If she had displayed the first two at her last job, she would still have it. With prompting, she revealed what little she knew of Lizette, who had preceded her at Singer by six months. Superficial information.

"Come, come, you knew her better than that!"

"I did?"

"A short memory for such a young woman. At Walter Martin," he coached.

Lily was all amazement.

"Buying fabrics for her personal wardrobe."

"If she came, it wasn't when I was there."

"You signed her in-on March 20th, April 2nd and May 10th.

Lily closed her eyes tight for a moment. She was going to kill Ted. "It's all a mistake."

"Is it?"

So she'd known Lizette before and lied about it. Not good.

"That's all for now, Miss Chasen, but-"

"I know, no vacations for a while. Don't worry, I can't afford any."

Lily left to join the others who hovered outside Bernard Singer's office.

"Ladies, please!" boomed Singer. "Get back to work! You'll be called when we're ready for you."

The group appeared to disperse as Margaret Singer approached to join Singer and Kirk. As the door swung nearly closed, the group reassembled to resume eavesdropping.

The commanding figure of Detective Inspector Kirk dominated the room. "A distressing situation for you, I'm sure, Miss Singer, but I must ask where you were at approximately 1:45p.m. yesterday afternoon."

"I was in my office, working on accounts receivable for Singer Couture. I was nowhere near that French floozie." The door slammed shut.

The women made a mad dash to the dressing room. One of them pressed the intercom connection to Bernard Singer's office.

"I don't like anyone who uses her body for advertising purposes, but I respected her, and all the girls, for doing their jobs well. I don't go around killing my nephew's employees."

"I was sure you wouldn't, but perhaps you could think of someone, not as high-minded as you, who might?"

"Certainly not," she snapped, "well, not at Singer, anyway. She had a man, boyfriend, I presume, who picked her up daily after work, an American. She had a French husband. What was she doing with an American? Our girls would die for a French husband [muted shrieks of outrage from the dressing room]. Most of them are unmarried."

"As are you."

"I'm not looking for a man!" came the indignant response.

"Just as well for the firm, of course. You might be distracted from your work."

"Nothing distracts me."

"Or escapes your notice?"

"Well-"

"Where were the other models at the time of the murder?"

"Their posted schedules make that clear."

"Not clear enough. I want you to verify to the best of your ability, the whereabouts of each model." Kirk produced a sheet of paper.

"I don't follow them around!"

"To the best of your ability. Perhaps some diverged from their schedules, left early to meet other commitments. And please indicate the same for the other employees." Another sheet appeared.

"I do not follow the janitors around to the toilets! But you might as well know, you'll find out anyway, that Patou girl, that's what they called her, was not well-liked by our models. Too French."

"Pardon?"

"Too French!"

◆ ◆ ◆

Ted was on time, his maroon Pontiac gleaming in the morning light.

"Thanks, Ted, I didn't get much sleep."

"I've told you; you can count on me any day and every day for a ride to work."

"Bad habit you've gotten into. What will all the girls eyeing you think?"

"That I'm not available."

"Oh, yes you are, and so am I. We're too young for a settled arrangements."

"The 'settled arrangement,' as you call it, is marriage. My mother was only eighteen when she signed up with Dad."

"I've spoken to your mother."

"Well, that's beside the point. It's the right thing to do."

"Talking about 'right things,' you could have let me know you signed Lizette in for me three times."

"I didn't want to bring that little lapse in your duties to your attention."

"So, I had to have Inspector Kirk bring it to my attention."

"I'm sorry, darling."

Lily glared at him.

"Dearest?"

Huge sigh.

"I didn't want Dad to fire you. I did as you asked and checked her account. She always paid by check, monthly, spread over the year. She still owes for four months."

"I hope your father isn't expecting to collect from a corpse."

"He might. They weren't her checks. They were signed by a Mr. Solomon Smith."

"So why have the police been following me for the past week?"

"Oh, they don't know about him. They only know she paid by check; they assumed it was hers."

"Ted!"

"Well, they didn't deserve to know, after what they put you through."

"They haven't been torturing me, Ted."

"So, you found the body, so what? So, you knew more about her than anyone else, and that wasn't much, so what? Anyone who could suspect you of murder isn't smart enough to find someone who is capable of it."

"Oh, no. Don't tell me you think you are."

"I am."

"How's your accounting class coming along?"

"I can't concentrate with you on my mind. When I find the murderer and you're in the clear, my classwork will improve dramatically."

"No, no, no!" screamed Lily's head. "Why must you always complicate my life, Ted!" echoed her heart. But aloud she growled,

"WE find the murderer."

"It's too dangerous for you-"

"-to let YOU run loose with this alone. Which bank were the checks written on?"

"Amalgamated on 34th Street. I'm hoping to have Mr. Smith's real name by this evening. I'll meet you for coffee at eleven at Schrafft's."

"No dinner, oh Lockinvar?"

"Yes, for Joan. She should be riffling the files now. An old girlfriend of mine. Too executive for my taste. Dad actually liked her." He pulled up in front of the home of Bernard Singer Couture, pecked her on the cheek and ran 'round to open her door. "No," he responded to the negative expression on her face. "I have to do this, for you, for us. At least consider my accounting class." He took a quick look around the relatively empty street, decided to forgo an unorthodox public kiss, slid over to the driver's seat, tipped his hat and was gone.

"Among other things, I am thinking of your accounting class, Ted," Lily mumbled as she entered the building. Any distraction from classwork would always be welcome. Ted hated accounting.

◆ ◆ ◆

"George Davenport?" Lily sipped her coffee.

"Yes, his father owned a string of garages all over the country. Made a fortune in ten years and died in '25. Junior sold them and left home base in Iowa City for parts unknown until he surfaced in New York City and met and married Sheila Wainwright, the only daughter of Wainwright Travel's Lionel Wainwright. Judging from his Davenport account at Amalgamated, he treats his wife like a queen. But why was he treating Lizette like a princess? He's only been married two years, too soon for boredom to set in."

"When does boredom set in, Mr. Husband-In-The-Making?" Ted's face reddened as he opened his mouth to respond. "Oh, never mind. I've heard of Mrs. Davenport. She hosts charity balls and luncheons, supports the arts, especially music and ballet. She's in the society columns all the time, but only since she married. She was a quiet appendage to her father, "mousy" is what I've heard her called, but when he died, about the time she met Davenport, she came into her own as head of Wainwright Travel. With a handsome, socially popular husband, I guess she feels she has to live up to the responsibilities of her new social position. What's the name of the family garage company?"

"Davenport Garages. Reasonable. What is it?"

Lily's gaze rested on two people across the room. "Nothing, nothing. Thanks for checking this out. Now I need some sleep."

Ted paid the bill and hurried after Lily, who was taking a long route to the exit.

"Don't worry, I'll talk to A'Lelia. It's not your fault." The elderly Negro man patted the hands of the young woman.

Lily smiled. "Hi," she said to the young woman as she passed her table. The woman was Tenisha Jones.

Chapter Four

Lily looked out the window of The Happiness Restaurant at The New York Public Library across the street, its steps flanked by lions. At least knowledge was defended.

"Why am I here?" asked a voice at her side. It was Tenisha Jones.

Lily smiled. "I thought you needed a little happiness."

"I need a drink." She sat and motioned to the waiter.

"I've got Ted Martin to blame for my predicament, but rumor has it your implication in Lizette's demise is more nefarious."

"Lizette bought beauty cream from Aunt A'Lelia. I'm supposed to be intimate with my wealthy aunt."

"What's criminal about wearing your aunt's beauty cream. Aren't White women allowed to buy it?"

"It was doctored, poisoned. It went through her skin to her entire body. Auntie won't be thrilled with me when she gets a visit from the police."

"They couldn't possibly suspect ---"

"No, they can't be that crazy, but she won't want her high-flying friends to hear even a whiff of scandal about anything she does. And I was hoping to persuade her to invite me to the gala she's holding in two weeks. There is someone on her guest list I would like to meet."

"What person would you like to meet?"

"Just someone. Why did you want me here?"

"Inspector Kirk's men are invading my privacy. Everywhere I look there's a man who quickly looks away, closes his newspaper, fumbles to light a cigarette."

Tenisha nodded.

"I don't know how long it will take for the police to follow more reasonable suspects, but I thought you might help me speed things up." She tilted her head toward the window. "The home of the lions can supply us with information that Detective Inspector Kirk doesn't have."

"How do you know that?"

"Uncle Harry's a desk sergeant. He knows where Inspector Kirk has been, and he hasn't been to The New York Public Library."

"What does he know?"

"This: Lizette Frere was the common-law wife of Charles Dupre. She came here after two years at Patou because she was fired for leaking his designs to a smaller design firm. Charles is now part owner and vice-president of the smaller firm, which sent them to New York with letters of introduction to Bernard Singer."

"Of course! His adaptations of French designs are more successful than the originals. A nice pair to saddle him with! What's the name of Dupre's company?"

"La Belle Femme."

"I've heard of them. They're having a show in October. We'll know soon how much of Singer Couture speaks French."

"And how much of Walter Martin is draped on those French mannequins. Why steal a little when you can steal a lot? Lizette bought fabrics from Walter Martin with checks signed by a

Solomon Smith, alias George Davenport, lately of Wainwright Travel fame."

"The Inspector knows this?"

"No, my darling Ted didn't tell him that Lizette didn't pay for the fabrics she bought for herself, or rather for La Belle Femme."

"Why don't you tell him?"

"And get Ted in trouble for withholding information? He was in a snit because I was a suspect. We'll need information on the Davenports, him and her. Since you've been sucked into this too, I thought you might consider helping me."

Tenisha was silent. She took another mouthful of scotch. "Why don't we leave this to the experts?"

"Exactly what I had in mind." Lily gazed out the window past the lions to the imposing steps and facade of The New York Public Library.

The women were swallowed up in the busy catalogue room. They took their book requests to the submissions desk in the cavernous reading room and sat at one of the long tables watching the miniature elevators behind the desk lumber up with request slips and down with the books. Tenisha broke the silence.

"I've often thought of going to France. Negro performers have a chance there, and Negro models, too."

"We have Negro performers here."

"They make their reputations in France, so they're welcome here unless they're models."

Two numbers flashed on the board at the desk.

"At least there's equality in the library," said Lily, as they went to retrieve their books. "Let's get through these before the next batch arrives."

An hour later they left the confines of "Silent Please" to share notes at The Happiness.

"Dupre was a hairdresser, including dressing wigs for stage appearances. Fashion wigs for fashion clothes. It wasn't lucrative enough, no big-name clients, so he joined his father's accounting firm. He'd studied accounting before he broke away and gravitated to hair. His future partner, Charles Terry, was one of his clients, so he combined business and the arts and broke away once more. La Belle Femme has been afloat for four years, but judging from its net figures, it's about to drown, despite rather good and increasing sales. Strictly couture, strictly expensive fabrics, strictly middle-class clientele. And since Charles Terry drank himself to death two years ago the company's been without a designer, an official designer, at least. Charles Dupre has referred to him simply as "our designer," probably an unknown. Maybe that's why the Patou borrowing has continued, at least until Lizette got fired. What have you found on Davenport, Ten?"

"He's a blank until two years ago, when he married Sheila Wainwright. He's not the Davenport of Davenport Garages. Here, look at this." She passed a newsprint picture to Lily. "Even without the moustache he'd be no Adonis. His weight and frame are similar to Wainwright's husband, though. After the sale, Mr. Garage Heir took off to travel to parts unknown and dropped out of the business headlines in Iowa, the firm's home state, until he turned up in social headlines here with Sheila Wainwright."

"It's odd, Ten, how Charles Dupre reacted to Lizette's death. What kind of husband, common-law or not, would say that he's not following her body back to France because he's got things to do here? That's what he told the newspapers."

"The police would not have let him go, anyway."

"But hardly a husband Singer models would die for, Margaret's opinion notwithstanding. Has Her Eminence told you the latest, Ten?"

"About Dupre?"

"About Dupre. Bernie is having a special showing of his spring line solely for him, using mainly Walter Martin fabrics."

"How did you ---"

"Ted."

"No such showing has been posted on the board."

"I know, but I don't think Bernie's going to model the clothes himself. If we can only be there and meet Dupre we can find out whether he knew about his competition and if his feelings toward Lizette had changed."

"We don't even know what those feelings were---a business arrangement with sex as a kicker or a deep personal commitment toward her."

"Since Margaret has you recording the schedules, you're bound to find out where and when. Ted won't tell me; I'm not sure he knows. He says he doesn't want me involved in the murder investigation any more than I am."

"I agree with him, and I don't want to get more involved either. This is police business. We're the only ones who know about the Davenport/Lizette and Dupre/Singer/Martin connections. We know too much. Uh, oh, that doesn't sound good."

"We'll have to talk to Davenport too, but it's more convenient to start with Dupre."

"You aren't listening. The police get paid to do this. I get paid to do office work and you get paid to model."

"But they've compromised your reputation."

"Only temporarily. I'd rather lose my reputation than my life."

"You said we already know too much. We can move ahead gingerly. Any idea why Singer Couture would want its line lifted by a small French firm?"

"If there's a contract, there's no lifting. If we can proclaim that we adapt French designs for the American market, why can't they want to proudly proclaim that they're adapting our designs for the French market? I'll find out what Margaret knows on Monday. Now, I've got to go. Saturday night is my total relaxation date with Donald, no cooking and no helping him prepare for course tests. First, I'll need a few hours to calm down and dress for an evening of dancing."

"Does he know about the murder case?"

"Very little. I have no interest in getting from him the kind of lectures I've given to you."

♦ ♦ ♦

"Margaret, has Mr. Singer made any changes to this week's schedule, any changes in models?"

"Why on earth should he? You know he rarely makes changes for the week in progress, and the girls have their other commitments. Did you see Margo's hands in the Van Raalte glove ad this morning? So lovely! We're sure to have them on loan for our spring show. Have all last week's purchases been escorted to their new homes?"

"All but Miss Henley's. She has an appointment with Joyce tomorrow to lower the hem. Inappropriate for her age, she says."

"Good. I've seen her knees. Don't forget the diet pastries for Mrs. Newman's fitting tomorrow morning."

"I've already ordered them."

"Splendid."

Half an hour later Lily Chasen stuck her head into Tenisha's tiny office. She spoke softly and distinctly.

"The showing for Dupre is tomorrow at noon, my friend."

" 'Friend' is definitely premature. Who's modeling?"

"I am."

Chapter Five

Lily listened to Bernard Singer explain the next day's unscheduled performances. Two days earlier he had seen her French textbook peeking out from under a pastry-topped napkin as she relaxed in the lounge. How admirable, he said, that she was studying the language of the land of fashion's source. Next, of course, she should study Italian. Fortunately, the language of the land of true fashion innovation, she already knew --- American English. He regretted having her model for a murder suspect, the suspicion, of course, being totally ridiculous, but her acquaintance with the French language would relax Mr. Dupre and allow him to express more easily how he proposed to use Singer's designs. The remuneration they would naturally discuss in private. The Singer brand acknowledged --- yes, it would have to be acknowledged, clearly acknowledged in Paris --- would be a coup of the first order.

"And why shouldn't France and America be on friendly terms, supporting each other as they did during revolutionary times? And our latest sojourner to France, aviatrix Ruth Elder, welcomed, applauded, feted!" Bernard Singer stopped for breath. "We have a chance for a special link to French couture, and we must not fail to make it. You must not fail to help." Singer looked at her expectantly.

"I will not fail to help." Lily slightly rolled her eyes, but Singer, fortunately, had turned away.

"Excellent! You must not speak of this to anyone. I haven't even told Margaret. You know how she felt about Lizette, how she feels about anything French, about fashion.... You'll take lunch at 2p.m. tomorrow, so eat a significant breakfast, please."

♦ ♦ ♦

Lily lay in bed and looked at the ceiling. Her apartment was such a wonderful refuge from the hectic fashion world, and such a tonic when she opened her eyes in the morning and they rested on the beautiful brocade of her bedside chair and the chiffon curtains, billowing slightly form the morning air, making her feel light as a feather and ready to start a joyous day. Half an hour later, she tiptoed barefoot across the floor, so as not to awaken the late riser downstairs. She wondered what he had thought of her bathtub rendition of "Sempre Libre," the emptying of the tub having drowned out the possibility of hearing any disapproval from below. With the towel around her shoulders, she headed for the closet. What to wear? She'd never gotten into the habit of laying out her clothes the night before. How could you be sure of the weather until you had listened to it on the radio that morning and stuck your head out the window to verify the report? How could you know the mood you would be in, or would like to be in? As she passed the entry door, she saw two sheets of paper slid under it. One, on the letterhead of Foster Electronics said "Very nice, but too loud." The other, on the back of a supermarket receipt had two taffy bars attached to it, along with the message, "I'll pick you up at 8:45. Is that all right?" Was she supposed to run down to the corner telephone in her slip to tell him if it weren't? Hadn't Ted told her to let him know if she wanted a ride to work? If he thought he was some sort of mind reader then he was wrong. She didn't want to lie if he asked about things Bernard Singer wanted private. Today blue skirt, white blouse and, oh, all right, one with some lace. Business-like and boring. She had a feeling there would be enough excitement to counter her look.

◆ ◆ ◆

Tenisha was at her desk wearing blue and white.

"You too? And so busy! Here, this will tide you over until lunch." She produced a taffy bar. "Courtesy of Ted."

A slight smile crossed Tenisha's face. A smile! thought Lily, as she checked her inbox. A confirmation of her hat shoot at Lilly Dache, a query from Kaiser Hosiery about her availability for a Vogue advertisement in two weeks, and an envelope with only her name on it and no return address. The handwriting was unmistakable. She reached for the arm of the settee at her side and sat down. She opened the envelope and unfolded the sheet of paper.

It said, "Urgent. Meet me in the lobby after work." It was signed "Lizette."

It was dated September 10th, the day of her death. Where had it been for ten days? Lily had last seen her alive ten minutes before she found her body. She had given no indication of any urgent need, but she had wanted to see her later, with no explanation given. She sniffed the envelope, then looked at the schedule board. She had a fitting for a dress in ten minutes and Sally for a suit in half an hour. She put the letter in her reticule and placed it in her locker before walking to the model's lounge. Ginger was imitating someone's walk and Sally was clapping her hands in delight.

"Sally, may I see you for a moment?"

Sally walked to the door, and Lily closed it behind her.

"How did you get that letter?"

"Letter?"

"Your perfume was on it."

"After my turn in the show, I dashed back to the dressing room to get some lemon throat drops. When I saw Lizette on the floor, I fell backwards into the table and knocked some things off.

I picked them up quickly and put them back, including the envelope, but when I saw her handwriting and that it was meant for you, and realized that it now had my fingerprints on it, and she looked dead, I decided to keep it and got out of there fast."

"Why didn't you give it to Inspector Kirk?"

"My boyfriend's a lawyer. It wouldn't look good for him if his girlfriend had a letter from the murder victim in her possession, and what doesn't look good for him isn't good for me."

"Why didn't you give it to me sooner?"

"I thought you might say I gave it to you, and I'd be implicated. It's from Lizette to you, that's all that should matter. Please don't look at me that way. I like you, but it was addressed to you. And I didn't steam it open, so I don't know what it says. You don't have to tell me if you don't want to."

"She said it was urgent that she meet with me that afternoon. I have no idea why."

"I suppose you're going to turn the letter over to the police. Please don't say I gave it to you. They'll probably think it's her perfume on the envelope."

"It's barely detectable now. No fragrance will be on it when I give it to them."

"When? You mean you won't do it right away? Gee, thanks!"

"Sally, I'm not doing this as a favor. You took ten days before you gave the letter to me. I need time to find an explanation for waiting ten days to give it to them, and make the truth sound believable! You're not involved, so don't mention this to anyone. I'm not involved either, but I am under suspicion, so what's one more piece of bogus evidence against me? You will be quiet about this?"

Vigorous assent. She clapped Sally on the shoulder and hurried to the fitting. Soon she would be off to rendezvous with Dupre and Singer.

Chapter Six

Lily hailed a taxi, no trolley day for her. She had to look fresh for the showing. The St. Regis was an impressive hotel. Even the lobby filled her with awe. She stopped at the desk to ask for directions. It was 11:30. Perhaps Singer had modeling instructions for her before the noon event. He greeted her at the door and pointed to a rack of clothes. A dozen outfits was rather a lot for one person to model without generous space between each presentation. Perhaps Singer and Dupre needed the time to discuss the clothes. Dupre did not appear until noon, giving Singer time to put his new shoes through their paces around the room.

"Greet him in French, and comment on the comfort of the clothes. Let your face register your pleasure with the styles." Singer had time to show her the clothes with commentary about the spring, 1928 collection he would unveil in January. La Belle Femme would unveil their version of Singer's collection in March. A distinguished -looking gentleman appeared at the door.

"Bonjour Monsieur Dupre!" Singer boomed, warmly clasping his hands. Lily's extended greeting in textbook French elicited a broad smile from the man, any broader and it might have metamorphosed into a laugh. She had been sure of the meanings of the words she chose, not so sure of how to express them grammatically. Dupre looked at each item of clothing carefully holding it up to room and window light before replacing it on the rack. His face registered neither approval nor disapproval. When he had finished, he waved the rack away, and Lily moved it behind the nearly ceiling high board that would serve as her dressing room.

"Commençons," he said, and Lily appeared in pink chiffon that hung loosely from her shoulders, with a belt in pink leopard-skin. Dupre pointed to the knee length, indicating he would raise it, and to the round collar, which would probably become a V-neck. Would that be all right? Singer indicated it would be all right in America, too. And so it went, Dupre explaining the changes La Belle Femme would probably make, and Singer consistently approving. Lily wondered how Dupre could be so sure that his nameless designer would agree to these changes, though the Frenchman did preface his remarks with "probably." Lily was in and out of clothes at breakneck speed, with barely time to arrange her hair in front of the six-foot mirror next to the chair she had no time to sit on. She admired Dupre's taste and his adaptations. She wondered how she could ask to speak to him about Lizette. For someone who was almost her husband, he had not mentioned her at all. Neither had Bernard Singer, but then it would be unseemly to put murder and fashion in close proximity. It was almost two o'clock, and the presentation was over. Dupre selected half the Singer collection for La Belle Femme, and Singer put the rest in the garment bags, so prying eyes would merely see a guest at The St. Regis departing with his wardrobe. But Dupre was not finished.

"May I speak to your model about my dear Lizette. She spoke fondly of her."

Singer was somewhat taken aback, but grateful that Lizette's demise had not affected their business transaction.

"Yes, yes, of course. When you're finished, Lily," he said, clearly indicating that more work at Singer Couture awaited her that day. A heartfelt handshake with the Frenchman and he was gone.

"We cannot talk here, Mr. Dupre. You and I alone in a hotel room is not acceptable in America. It's past lunchtime for most New Yorkers. We should be able to talk in privacy in the hotel restaurant. Besides, I'm starved!"

♦ ♦ ♦

As the waiter went off to get her salad, she began. "It must be hard for you. Lizette spoke of you so often."

"Yes, I miss her so! But I've a business to run and can't stay. I want her murderer found. She said the other models were jealous of her."

"Perhaps, but committing murder would hardly enhance their reputations, which are all-important to them."

"What about the horrid business manager and her assistant, the one who rarely talks?"

"Anyone could possibly have done it, but the probability of Mr. Singer's aunt and her assistant doing it aren't great. However, the police are suspicious of everyone. In time they're bound to discover who murdered your Lizette."

"Yes, and to also discover things that are none of their business, things that can ruin people's lives. There's a Mr. Davenport; he's in the business news often. Our company didn't have money for samples of the best fabrics, so I asked Lizette to make his acquaintance, to be nice to him, so that he would buy her fabrics he thought she would use to make her own clothes. We settled on Walter Martin Fabrics because of the designs and quality. It was simpler than spreading Davenport's checks around the fabric world. He would think she had a favorite fabric house.

"She thought he was getting too interested in her, and toward the end, when we had the fabrics we wanted, she started bringing his wife into their conversations. He knew that she had a lover back home, and he may have felt she was dropping him after he'd spent so much on her. He didn't know that I was in New

York, or that Lizette was leaving with me when I returned to Paris. Is it possible that he ---" Dupre swallowed hard and looked away from Lily. "Maybe he told his wife he was leaving her and she did it. All his money gone. A settlement, yes, but a public disgrace. I've been reading about her. She's not a lady likely to accept this, and her looks are not likely to attract another wealthy man."

"You haven't told the police about Mr. Davenport?"

"No, if he's not the murderer there's no good to come from linking La Belle Femme to a disloyal husband, at least not in America, and we have our reputation here in the future to consider. Lizette said you were the only model she liked and trusted. I'd be grateful for your help."

"What would you like me to do?"

"You have a link with two companies Lizette had dealings with. Your boyfriend has the inside track at Walter Martin. Mrs. Davenport has bought fabrics in the past from Martin, or her dressmaker has for her. Could Mr. Ted Martin investigate her and her husband, and could you see what you can find out at Singer that might shed light on who could possibly have murdered her? It's asking a lot and it's certainly not your line of work, I know, but she liked you and you liked her, and she was my Lizette. "

"You realize the police think you had a motive, too."

"They're grabbing at any possibility, even the most ludicrous. We can't increase our purchases at Walter Martin, but we can have him design fabrics especially for us. We could talk to Mr. Ted Martin, work it out with him."

"Some would call this bribery."

"Not at all. Original fabrics, ours alone, would set us apart. Mr. Martin would have a presence in France."

Walter Martin is not Bernard Singer, thought Lily. A touch of murder would seriously curb his desire for a French connection.

"You are the face of La Belle Femme, Mr. Dupre, but you are not the designer. Does he agree to your proceeding this way?"

"He agrees. At least think about doing what I ask. You can reach me at this address and at this number in New York City."

He pulled an elegant business card and a pen from his pocket and proceeded to neatly record the information. He shook her hand in parting. It was a strong handshake, and as Lily headed for the trolley back to work, no need to pamper herself with a taxi now, she flexed her fingers to restore the circulation.

♦ ♦ ♦

She passed Tenisha's office en route to a fitting, and the young Negro woman motioned her inside.

"My aunt pooh-poohed the whole thing. She said that anyone could have doctored Lizette's face cream. She said all the girls here who used her cream should check theirs. A drop of it in half a glass of water will reveal if it's safe. A color change means trouble."

"I'm fine. I don't use it."

"I won't tell auntie that."

"I suppose you're no longer interested in the case. You're not much of a suspect, and your aunt's pretty much in the clear."

"If I'm not involved, I can't be interested?"

"Well, there's no reason to involve yourself in what could be a dangerous situation."

"Maybe I admire your determination."

"That's one of the nicest things you've ever said to me. Actually, it's one of the few things you've ever said to me."

"I don't like to talk much at work. Everyone's so self-oriented, so selfish. But you seem to care."

"About what?"

"People."

A bit of pink suffused Lily's cheeks. "Dupre tried to bribe me with business for Ted if I would, well, essentially solve the murder for him. He said he doesn't think that the police are up to it."

"That's suspicious. Dupre wants a model with operatic training to solve a murder?"

"He claims it's his love for Lizette and justice, but I'm thinking that with Lizette as the linchpin between Walter Martin Fabrics, Bernard Singer Couture and Paris, her murder may have business implications, even that her death may be the forerunner of others."

"Not ours, I hope."

"You mean you'll work with me?"

"Don't ever think of going in for public relations. You'll talk all potential clients out of a relationship. Where do you suggest we start?"

"With this." Lily handed her the letter that Sally had belatedly given her. "It was on the table in the dressing room. Sally knocked what was on the table to the floor. When she saw this letter, now with her fingerprints on it, she panicked, kept it, and just gave it to me yesterday. She saw the body before I did, but I got the 'credit' for it."

"Like Columbus getting credit for discovering America when the discoverer was Americus Vespucci. My boyfriend's a history major. I'm trying to find some use for the information he shovels at me."

"History, that's what we need. We've got some background on Dupre and La Belle Femme, and Singer's and Martin's histories are open books, but Davenport is a blank, and his French connections seems to begin and end harmlessly, Mrs. Davenport's sensibilities aside, with Lizette. Could–"

"Donald."

"Could Donald find out, for starters, who he is? We know he's not the garage Davenport. If Donald could research his photo maybe he'd come up with something."

"I think it would be a stretch for Donald. He's got papers to write and tests to prepare for, and I don't think I could persuade him that it's any of his business. We may have to let the police take care of this, once you tell them about Davenport. If you wait much longer you may find that you've dug a hole for yourself that doesn't presently exist. While we're waiting for the good inspector to produce information on Davenport and for your uncle-sergeant to tell you about it, we can draw preliminary conclusions about the man once I've met him. I asked Aunt A'Lelia if he and his wife were coming to her party next week. She said no, but she'd send a handwritten, hand-delivered invitation to them. They're not likely to refuse a chance to attend one of the great A'Lelia Walker's social events. 'This is exciting!' she said. She wants me there to meet them and report back to her. We'll see about 'report back.' Now, what am I going to wear?" Tenisha drummed her fingers on the desk.

"At the party, try to be charming. Well, be yourself, or maybe --"

"Maybe you should dress up in blackface and go in my place!"

Lily laughed. "I'm off to the fitting."

"Hey, be careful what you tell Inspector Kirk. The truth of course, all of it, Sherlock, but word it carefully. If leads are few, he's likely to pounce on any unfortunate phrasing. Will you have time to plan your little speech?"

"What, I can't think and have a fit at the same time?"

Chapter Seven

Lily looked over the sheet music with pleasure. She didn't mind creating lyrics that suited particular Singer clothes, but she was delighted when some of the popular songs were a match for some of the fashions. The rack Dupre had examined was now in the showroom, and Lily was matching potential best-selling clothes to best-selling songs. Off-stage Susie was creating chords for the lyrics just written and would soon be ready to run through the songs Lily was now selecting. Bernard Singer strode briskly toward her, his large expanse of gray-streaked hair dancing on his head.

"Well, what musical delights will we spring on buyers in January, Lee?" He called to Susie to illustrate Lily's originals, pulling out the indicated clothes and waving them from side to side and to and fro in mock runway fashion, then on to the songs beloved by millions.

"Perfect! Perfect! You are a treasure!" He kissed Lily lightly on the cheek.

"Bernie, why did you hire me?"

"You know why. You had the model's figure I needed, the voice I wanted for singing and Miss Revilier hadn't arrived."

"But if you wanted a singer, why didn't you use Lizette?"

"Lizette could sing? Charles didn't tell me that, only that he thought a French model would enhance perception of our line, and it certainly has, and now, with our fashions soon to debut in Paris, we're on the verge of an international reputation. It's an honor that he chose our House."

"Then La Belle Femme is a fashion house of some note in Paris?"

"It's small, but respected. Oh, when you do that glove ad for Kaiser next week, let me know if the hype is justified. I'm thinking of buying a pair for my wife."

"They'd love to include that in their ad copy!"

"And we could use more glove loans for our showings."

No fingerprints on gloves, thought Lily. When had Lizette last worn gloves? But she had been poisoned through her face cream. Now there was no Lizette to offer advice, to chat with about clothes, makeup, men. Lily missed her.

♦ ♦ ♦

"I assumed you were aware of most of this, but I wanted to get some of it off my mind."

"Is there more on your mind, Miss Chasen?" asked Inspector Kirk.

Unfortunate phrasing, thought Lily. "Only that I liked Lizette and want her murderer found. Nothing I said surprised you?"

"No, some new information, but no surprises. Are you sure that's all you want to tell me?"

"What more is there to tell?"

"You profess a desire to sing opera, but you give no recitals."

"I'm not ready."

"You take no lessons."

"I did take some, I just can't afford more at the moment."

"You give no indication of actually pursuing an opera career."

Lily stared at Inspector Kirk. He was right, but if he was implying a nefarious purpose in working at Bernard Singer Couture, then he was wrong.

"If I can help you in any way..." Lily's voice trailed off.

"No, my dear, but if any more letters or information should come your way, I would be grateful if you would let me know. Otherwise, I'm quite capable of investigating a murder."

CHAPTER EIGHT

The chandeliers shimmered in rainbow hues. Aunt A'Lelia's mother had wanted the best, so Austrian crystals glittered overhead. For an eight o'clock event Tenisha had arrived twenty minutes late, respectful and respectable, though the eighty-odd people already chatting and drinking made it clear that arriving on time was totally acceptable. Her pink satin wrap was taken by a man in tails and placed on a hanger on one of the makeshift racks behind the marble table in the vast foyer of the Irvington estate. Her pink satin skirt, just below the knee and the limp white satin blouse felt right. As she hesitated at the entrance to the ballroom, Aunt A'Lelia bore down on her.

"So glad you're here, darling. Come with me." She steered her niece to modeling agency superstar John Robert Powers, introduced her to him and hurried off to a pretend call from across the room. The Powers girls were all the rage, to sell a hat, a suit, a dress, to sell an image the public wanted, a beautiful woman at ease with herself, comfortable in her skin and in whatever she was wearing. The Powers girls were quickly recognized. They were the everywoman that every woman wanted to be. They were not Tenisha Jones. But perhaps Powers would be interested in someone beyond the mold, someone with an elegant European flair, like Josephine Baker, the rage of

Europe, despite her American roots. Negro women did, after all, buy clothes. Powers was polite and attentive. Negro women did indeed buy clothes, and Tenisha's suggestion deserved serious consideration. Tenisha smiled wanly. Serious consideration in a hostile social environment was like sending a bill for further study to a government committee, in which it stayed for a lifetime. Suddenly, Aunt A'Lelia was at Tenisha's elbow.

"Mr. Powers, someone is most anxious to speak with you. I assume that you do not carry grudges and are willing to reservice a former client on a greater scale than before."

Powers laughed. "Of course."

"Then do come with me."

The room was awash with movement and color, and with it came a modicum of socializing to bind together the goal of the evening --- growing a business or a career. A'Lelia Walker's guests were predominately in the arts, and as she worked her way back to Tenisha, she left in her wake wheels turning, connections made and new possibilities in the offing. Without a word she took Tenisha's hand and led her to a dashing, young man it was hard to miss; his was the only white evening jacket in a sea of black tuxedos.

"Mr. Davenport, my niece Tenisha. She's been dying to meet someone with your clothes sense, so individualistic, so refreshing. Oh," she exclaimed, past Davenport's shoulder, looking at a corner of the ballroom where nothing unusual was happening, "You must excuse me." Davenport reached out a hand for Tenisha's. His grip was strong.

"My! You must have worked on automobiles as well as run a garage empire!" Vehicles were a good opening, she thought, and they chatted for a while about them.

"I've dreamed over many Wainwright Travel brochures, but I expect that the travel business, even without my active participation, is booming since Ruth Elder's return from France."

"We were doing very well before her remarkable flight, but she has enhanced our bottom line. And your business is ---?"

"Business management at Bernard Singer Couture."

"Ah, a sad event there of late. I imagine you are all struggling to get past it."

"Her face cream was doctored."

"Good heavens, so that's what it was. The newspapers made no mention of it."

"Oh, I shouldn't have said anything. And it was Aunt A'Lelia's cream, too."

"Oh, dear! Not the kind of publicity her wonderful company needs! I shall not repeat it, of course."

"Thank you, Mr. Davenport. I'd much appreciate it. And we appreciate that Mrs. Davenport occasionally honors Singer with her patronage. We hope that won't stop."

"My wife is quite the fashionista. I try to look as impressive in my clothes as she does in hers, but as you can see," his right hand swept the room, "the impression I make may not be the one I would prefer."

"I must tell you frankly that I am not used to attending one of my aunt's grand affairs, and though I can coordinate our clients, I'm not certain I coordinate myself properly for such elegant events."

"Oh, you mustn't feel that way. One must start somewhere, and you've started very well. The two shades of satin blend beautifully, and the cut and style are quite elegant. My wife taught me all I know. Now if I would only practice it! May I get you a drink?"

"No, thank you. I see my aunt waving me away, so I'll not monopolize your time. I do want the privilege of coming to auntie's estate again. So nice to have met you."

Davenport laughed and heartily shook her hand. What her aunt had been waving was a handkerchief at Duke Ellington, whose band was now seated and visible to all on the risers that had been set up near the French doors that led to the garden. With her aunt's signal to begin, they did just that, with the rousing "Hop Head." Couples quickly filled the dance floor, swinging with abandon to the irresistible music. Of those unable or unwilling to cavort to the Duke's composition, one person stood out. Farthest from the band, she was the center of attention of a clutch of women. Her calm, aristocratic demeanor was at odds with the electricity the band was generating. Her fashion sense was impeccable, but she would have looked good regardless, her easy movements and assurance and elegant carriage making negligible the fact that she was not a physically beautiful woman. Tenisha accepted a canapé and a drink and, fortified by both, approached Mrs. Davenport. An upcoming charity event was the point of discussion. Tenisha waited patiently for a conversation opening.

"Pardon me, but I must express my admiration for the work you do for society's less fortunate members. I'm Tenisha Jones, Aunt A'Lelia's niece."

"Thank you so much. It's my pleasure to do whatever I can. Are you involved in charity work?"

Only for myself, thought Tenisha, but she said, "Not at the moment."

"Oh," said Mrs. Davenport, in what was an unmistakable dismissal.

"But Bernard Singer would like to sponsor a showing of his spring collection for one of your charities."

"Oh!" responded Mrs. Davenport, her earlier dismissal dismissed. "Which charity?"

"Mr. Singer leaves that for you to decide."

"I thought you looked familiar. How exciting! He's so innovative in translating French fashion for the American market. I would be delighted to work with him on such an event. Do thank him for me, and tell him I'll be in touch this week."

"Perhaps you might involve some men in the fashion selection process: Women's Clothes Through Men's Eyes."

"What an interesting idea."

"Your husband seems rather knowledgeable. He said you taught him all he knows."

"That's hardly a compliment." She laughed. "His understanding of women's fashion is nil, and he has absolutely no interest in it. Explaining to him why a suit is attractive is like pouring water down a sieve. All my darling knows is that if I'm wearing it it's gorgeous, because I'm gorgeous." She laughed again. "Besides, he's colorblind."

◆ ◆ ◆

"Apparently her fashion knowledge has rubbed off on him, but just as apparently he hasn't let her know." Tenisha took another sip of coffee. "Walking through a roomful of strangers is bearable if you're holding a glass of spirits, but not if you feel obliged to drink from it. Unfortunately, a glass to the lips when you don't want to answer a question is the best delaying tactic. My head is almost back to normal." She rubbed her forehead.

"Ten, you're the best! And you don't even have to do this."

"Don't remind me. Well, what do you think?"

"Mr. Davenport does seem to understand fashion, but maybe he doesn't want to step into his wife's territory and open himself to fashion talk, the bane of most men, if Ted and my father are examples of the sex. But he did buy the fabrics from Walter Martin for Lizette and 'apparently,' that dangerous word again, knew what he was buying, but did he know why he was buying it for her, that it was going to La Belle Femme? Did he personally know Dupre? Was he involved in any way with his fashion house? Was his attachment to Lizette business, personal or a combination of both?"

"Maybe she was modeling a dress he bought for his wife when he went to Paris on Wainwright Travel business."

"There are too many maybes, Ten. And what about that Davenport in the news story? Is that his brother?"

"Do you remember the date of the article?"

"January 20,1925. When did he leave Iowa for New York?"

"There's no newspaper record of that, only that his wife met him at the party he crashed on May 10, 1925. He could have been floating around New York for about four months, looking for something more interesting to do than run a garage empire."

"If he did run one. We don't know that he knows anything about garages or cars."

"Yes, we do." Tenisha pulled a folded paper from her purse. "This is for Ted. As I was scrambling for conversation, I remembered Ted's new Pontiac. These are Davenport's tips for maintaining the vehicle and some of the quirks Ted can expect to surface and what to do about them. By the time he finished talking, I could understand why he wanted to be in another business!"

"Of course, the company he's running now is his father-in-law's. Lucky the woman he married had it at hand."

"He certainly had the money to start one from scratch, Lee."

"If he really was the heir to a string of garages. But what do we know about him that we can verify? Only that romantic story of his meeting his wife and their social and business successes since."

"That's all the public wants to know --- a fairytale romance of a handsome, dashing, wealthy man with a plain-looking woman. Wonderful dreaming material for lots of ordinary-looking ladies."

"No one can say he married her for her money, Ten, but more important, she can't say it."

"And she certainly has a trail of articles linking her to this or that Don Juan, but nothing came of any of it. They had the social cachet, but no money. Remember that headline, 'I Will Only Marry for Love'? Well, love should be a two-way street, and she held out for it."

"If Lizette was worried that Davenport was getting serious with her, maybe his wife only got a one or one and a half way street. We need more information. Let's find out how Handsome behaved in his garage days. Let's contact his family."

"Are they likely to share such information with a stranger?"

"No, Ten, but at Walter Martin's I recall seeing some invoices from clients in Iowa. Possibly Ted went there on business and parked his new car in one of their garages. Possibly it got nicked."

"So Ted's Pontiac will be our entrée to Davenport's brother. You're sure Ted will do this?"

"Why not. He can make an appointment from the comfort of his home, instead of stuffing nickels into a telephone down the block. He's been clamoring for me to get a telephone for safety reasons, but I'm saving my money. I'm safe enough."

Tenisha raised an eyebrow. "Does Ted ever say 'no' to you?"

"Not within my hearing."

Chapter Nine

The models, in various stages of dishabille, huddled together around Margo, who was reading aloud the New York Times article they had all read over and over days before. The flying icon was really coming to Singer Couture!

"Girls! We begin in five minutes!" stated Singer firmly. If Miss Elder arrived on time they surely would. An exclamation from the window sent them all rushing to it. On the street below a limousine had stopped.

"She's here!"

A female, nattily dressed, one could tell even from the second floor, placed one leg outside the door the driver had opened, followed it with the other, was assisted to the sidewalk and entered the building.

"She's on her way up!"

The vibrating chime that announced the eminent rang softly in the Singer foyer.

"She's arrived!"

The models made a beeline for the wings. At Singer's nod Tenisha Jones stepped back, allowing him to open the door and greet the star with a flourish, a bow, and a "Welcome, welcome, my dear Miss Elder." Rick, in tails, took her coat, and Andy, also in tails, placed caviar on the lone, round marble table in the showroom and poured the champagne as Singer escorted his guest to one of the two red velvet chairs he only retrieved from storage for royalty. Sue, in sequins behind the Steinway, began soft music that would not detract from the brief conversation that would precede the showing.

"A salute to you, Miss Elder," said Bernard Singer raising his glass, "to your courage, your spirit, your achievement."

"But she didn't make it through to Paris," whispered Sally.

"She tried," said Margo. "Could she help it if The American Girl developed an oil leak? She's as brave as Charles Lindbergh to me."

"I'm so pleased," said Singer, "that you chose to visit us upon your return. That you could even think of us, of any American fashion house in the midst of the celebrations for your flight and your safe return honors us greatly."

"Besides my passion for flying, fashion is a major interest for me, and before I return to Florida, my husband is impatient for our return, I knew I had to visit the couture house on the cutting edge of fashion here. When the amazing La Belle Femme recommends American competition, there is no other choice."

"Thank you," said Singer, beaming. "I've assembled a range of clothing, as you requested. Any color or fabric changes you want will be effected immediately, but each piece is currently available in your size; we did not wish to keep you waiting."

"Thank you. I'm anxious to wear 'America' for the parties and celebrations this city has so kindly and graciously arranged in my honor. The mayor himself, whom the French adore, has been the epitome of kindness and, I must say it, flattery about my person and my deeds. Next time I intend to complete the flight to Paris."

"We do not doubt your determination or your skill. The country --- the world, I must say --- is in awe of you."

"Too kind," she murmured, and looked at the runway.

Singer raised a finger, and the music began. Sue at the Steinway was all that was needed. No sung words of persuasion were necessary. This woman knew her mind and her taste. This, after all, was Ruth Elder. Francois read straightforward descriptions of the clothes and their component parts, adding a discreet French accent to Singer's American clothes. In thirty minutes, it was over, and Miss Elder prepared to leave with her choices. That very night she would wear the gown that Ginger had modeled. She paused at the door. She had not seen Lizette. George Coulet, President of La Belle Femme, had asked her to convey his best wishes to his former model, who had been seduced by the glamor of New York and fashion's Bernard Singer Couture. Singer, flustered, searched for an explanation.

"A fatal attack felled the poor girl," Tenisha burst in.

"Yes, we've sent our condolences to all who loved her." Singer looked gratefully at Tenisha.

"Oh, my," exclaimed Miss Elder, a hand clasped to her breast. "In the midst of life... We must make the most of it. Indeed, we must, we must."

"And she shall," murmured Tenisha, as Bernard Singer escorted her to the elevator and to the street below. "She must have plenty of money to afford the beauties she just carried away."

Margaret's look was echoed by a verbal reprimand. "We don't charge patriots of her caliber for mere clothes," she said proudly. "Besides," she said more softly, "she's a walking advertisement for Bernard Singer Couture."

"Big bucks coming this way," said Tenisha. "Maybe we'll even get a raise." The young women laughed.

Margaret turned on them and in shocked tones said, "I'm surprised at you, Tenisha!"

"I'm even beneath being reprimanded," whispered Lily, as she and Ten grabbed their coats and hurried to the stairs.

"Forget your vanity, Lee. Ruth Elder may have information we can use. Where is she staying?"

"Same place as Charles Dupre, The St. Regis."

"Everyone who's anyone or wants to be stays there. I wonder how La Belle Femme is handling his absence from Paris?"

"I had Ted call the company and ask for him, and they said he was away."

"They just want to distance themselves from murder."

They were at the corner now.

"Here's my bus. Come home with me, Ten. I've got a roast chicken in the refrigerator. Ted will drive you home later. If you're really committed to this adventure, we've got to talk."

Chapter Ten

"Relationships, Ten. From the center out." Lily reached behind for a pencil and pad on her desk and drew a circle in the middle of the first sheet. She labeled it "Lizette." She drew rays outward from the center and labeled them Davenport; Dupre; Wainwright; Martin; models; Singer, B and Singer, M.

"The Singers? Margaret can be nasty, even vicious, but a murderer? And Bernard? Well, he is ambitious, but..."

"They're suspects, only suspects. Notice I left us out."

"Thanks!"

"If we look at these relationships from Lizette's point of view, we have a better chance of understanding how the goals, purposes and viewpoints of the others agree with or conflict with hers."

"So, the centerpiece is Lizette, and her effect on the others. What brought you to this line of thinking?"

"Ruth Elder. Did you read this?" Lily held up a copy of the November 12th Herald Tribune.

"No, I read the New York Times article."

"Well, listen to this, and map this out for Ruth Elder." She tore a sheet from the pad awaiting the "Lizette" map, and drew a circle with the icon's name and long rays emanating from it labeled with the people in her life mentioned in the article. "She'll be our practice centerpiece map, and even if you're impatient—"

"I am."

"---the process is important enough to do right. Besides, the article is a hoot! Add adjectives on each ray reflecting the person involved with Miss Elder. Any comments about Ruth herself write in the circle. I'll read slowly. Ready?"

Tenisha cut herself another slice of apple pie and poured herself another cup of coffee. "Ready."

Ruth Elder came back to New York yesterday. Not the typical American Girl of boyish swagger dressed in English cut plus fours, an English broadcloth sport shirt and a Scotch plaid necktie, but the typical American girl who wears French tailored clothes charmingly.

At her heels saying that all the shouting was for her the quiet birdman who was the pilot of the Stinson Detroiter American Girl at its attempt at a non-stop flight from New York to Paris.

Heroes despite their failure to span the Atlantic by air Miss Elder and George Haldeman returned aboard the Cunard Aquitania as heroes. The city officially greeted them.... They left a month and a day ago....

One of the first persons to greet Miss Elder when she stepped on board the municipal steamer was her husband, Lyle Womack. He had parried all questions about his wife's plans although nervously admitting he would like to take her back to a domestic role in their home in Panama [Florida]. In the rush of excitement which swept over the boat when Miss Elder and Haldeman boarded it, he got lost momentarily in the crowd. After posing for pictures on the bridge, Miss Elder and her co-pilot went into the cabin for an interview

with newspapermen. It turned out to be a three-cornered affair with a theatrical press agent answering not a few of the leading questions.

"Have you signed any theatrical or motion picture contracts?"

"No, not yet," answered Miss Elder, while the press agent gazed fascinated at his fingertips.

"Are you going to do any more flying?"

"I certainly hope to." Someone looked around for Mr. Womack, but he was nowhere to be seen.

"Will you be content to go back to Panama and wash dishes for your husband?"

"I have washed dishes," was the noncommittal answer.

"Do you plan to try a non-stop flight to Paris again?"

"I hope I shall be able to. I shall never be completely satisfied until I have, and have succeeded."

With ease and much poise, Miss Elder answered the questions put to her. She wore a small black hat, a black broadcloth coat trimmed in gray fur over a dark sports suit. She repeatedly denied that she had signed any contracts and said that she had not discussed one with Joseph Schenk, who was a passenger on The Aquitania. She sat back and smiled when it came Haldeman's turn to be interviewed.

"Mr. Haldeman, are you going to fly the Atlantic again?"

"That depends."

"Would you fly with Miss Elder again?"

"That depends."

[Lily jumped ahead and off the boat.]

Mayor Walker beamed approvingly when the girl flyer was formally presented to him by Mr. Whalen and in his extemporaneous address of welcome, he referred three times to her charm and beauty.

"Your confidence in the resourcefulness, in the courage and in the chivalry of Captain Haldeman has been justified and vindicated," said the mayor. "His confidence in your courage, your poise and your ability to face a crisis if necessary has also been justified. The courage of Captain Haldeman cannot be magnified nor exaggerated. Other men have crossed, made non-stop flights, but that a man should have such an understanding of womanhood that he would take one as a companion in this perilous task is another tribute to the confidence the American man has in American womanhood."

"He's delusional." Lily laughed. "What are your mapping conclusions?"

"I threw in a touch about her background, is that all right?"

"Fine."

"Ruth Elder has her act together. She knows what she wants, and she intends to get it. She 'hopes' to fly again, 'hopes' to try nonstop to Paris again, shall never be completely satisfied (whoever is) until she does and succeeds, but her expectation is that she will sign a motion picture/theater contract, that's a given. It hasn't happened 'yet,' but it will, and then this attractive, charming, former stenographer and dental assistant, who's already at ease in the spotlight, will never have to wash dishes again, and her quiet co-pilot and nervous husband can just get lost!"

Lily laughed again. "With your analytical powers applied to mapping Lizette and the people in her life, we should be well on our way to discovering her murderer."

"The problem is we can't do for Lizette what I just did for Ruth Elder. Elder was the centerpiece of her celebration, but Lizette is not the centerpiece of her murder. How others related to the centerpiece is important, but Lizette is merely one of the "others" who was a threat to the centerpiece."

"Then anyone at Singer, La Belle, or who knows where could be the centerpiece. How do we map an unknown?"

"We can make each suspect, in turn, the centerpiece. Davenport is the biggest unknown. Why don't we start with him?"

Lily quickly created a relationship map with George Davenport at its center. She and Ten stared at it.

"We don't have enough information for this. Even Uncle Harry's input doesn't give us enough to work with. The police haven't gotten very far with the case."

Tenisha picked up the pencil and drew another ray. She labeled it Ruth Elder. "They don't know about her, and she's a neutral party. Maybe something she knows about Lizette will relate to Davenport, or another potential centerpiece."

"We've got to talk to her before she heads back to Panama. No," she stopped Tenisha from speaking, "I need you with me. I'm just a model, but you represent the firm; you assist our finance guru, Margaret, you organize appointments and greet clients; yes, you."

"You bring home twice my income, but you're just a model."

"Don't be petty. At times like this I wish I had a telephone. It's getting dark, and I don't feel like running down to the corner." She walked to her dressing table for an atomizer of Chanel No. 5, and took it to her desk. She sprayed a sheet of writing paper, took a pen and wrote.

"Tell me if you like the éclairs from that new pastry shop. They're in the refrigerator. I'll be right back." She walked down a flight of stairs and pushed the sheet under a door. The note read: "Dear, dear Mr. Foster, may I use your telephone? Lily."

Chapter Eleven

"We appreciate this audience with you, Miss Elder."

Tenisha gave Lily a strange look. "Audience?" Should they be bowing?

"The tragedy of Lizette's death haunts us all at Bernard Singer Couture, and Mr. Singer would be grateful for any light you can shed on Lizette. If we can help the police close the case on this horrible murder, we want to do it. The police are not aware that you patronized La Belle Femme, and why should they be at this dazzling moment in your life? Why subject you to questioning about a case that has nothing personally to do with you? But if you could help us, informally, give us any recollections you have about La Belle Femme, Mr. George Coulet, his comments about Lizette, you may be instrumental in seeing that justice is done for a young woman who had a bright future before her."

"I'd be glad to help, but I don't think what I know matters."

"La Belle Femme is a small fashion house. What brought you there?"

"Since Patou is all the rage, I went there first. During the course of a few hours, several of the employees mentioned an 'upstart' firm that was copying their styles at lower prices and winning an audience among the French middle class. When I responded that Patou could sue them and stop the theft, they replied that it wasn't quite theft, that they did have original designs, but some of them were too close to theirs, and that they had six months earlier fired a model who knew the principals at La Belle Femme, because they believed she was leaking their designs to that firm. I expressed surprise that a model would be aware of planned designs, but they said they could not otherwise account for the similarities at La Belle Femme. I realized that while my Patou fashions would turn heads now in our country, I could be on the cutting edge of fashion by acquiring some clothes from the smaller fashion house."

"And were the clothes at La Belle Femme what you expected?"

"Oh, they exceeded my expectations. I saw the faintest of Patou touches, but otherwise the clothes were delightfully different, chic, fairy-tale gorgeous and oh, so feminine! And practical, too. They didn't stain at a mere glance, or so they told me, and looking at their scintillating collections of suits, dresses, blouses, skirts and evening gowns, I was more than willing to believe them!"

"Do you know where they got those fabrics?"

"From America, would you believe it! Mr. Coulet said that their clothes are not, at present, available in the United States, but that Bernard Singer Couture is an imaginative American design house with which they hope to join forces and which uses the same fabulous fabrics. Naturally, I couldn't resist visiting your establishment to see for myself, and Mr. Coulet was right!"

"What did he say about Lizette?"

"Only that he would like me to send her his best wishes. He obviously had affection for her because he proudly showed me pictures of her modeling their clothes and standing between him and another man, their arms around her shoulders and hers around their waists. He showed pictures of her modeling clothes he said she had introduced at their seasonal showings. He seemed very proud of her."

"Was she wearing a marriage ring in the photos?"

"You know, I didn't notice, but his manner when he spoke of her indicated a close attachment, to the firm at least."

"What did George Coulet look like?"

"Oh, very handsome, and very charming. Full face, soft blue eyes, a magnificent physique, his shirt unbuttoned almost to his waist. I kept thinking that his clothes could be less fabulous and women would still buy them because they were his!"

"A dream Frenchman, then?"

"A dream everyman. He didn't look particularly French, and his English, fortunately for me, was very good."

"And the other man in the picture?"

"Mr. Coulet didn't say who he was, but he was good-looking too, in a more European way. Tall, slim, debonair."

"On your next trip to France, perhaps another amazing nonstop flight, I assume you'll be back for more clothes."

"If I can afford them! Mr. Coulet was very kind in allowing me to have model samples of his latest fashions. But I'm hoping I won't have to wait that long to acquire more beautiful French clothes. I'm thrilled with my exquisite Singer creations, but if there is some sort of La Belle Femme and Singer Couture relationship in America, I will be able to get the best of both worlds, and if certain contracts I contemplate signing come to pass, I should be able to afford them. Now I really must end this interview. There's so much more to do before I leave, before my husband and I leave for home."

Miss Elder turned off the light in the conference room The St. Regis had allowed her to use, pointing in the corridor to the awesome ceiling, period wallpaper and tables, and beautiful sculptures. "I'm so blessed," she said.

At the far end of the lobby a man wearing a white muffler was looking at his watch. He turned toward the door. With a sharp intake of breath Ruth Elder called out, "Mr. Coulet!" But the man redoubled his steps and made a speedy departure without turning toward her.

"Amazing! I saw him in Paris not more than two days ago. This must mean that the Coulet/Singer relationship is already under way!"

"Are you sure it was Coulet?" asked Lily.

"Oh, yes, no doubt of it. I'm afraid my voice is too ladylike for even my shouts to be heard."

You were loud enough, thought Lily, as she looked at the smattering of guests in the lobby, the photographers who had laid in wait for Miss Elder's return from the partying and celebrations that had filled her day and early evening, long gone. She turned to Tenisha in time to see her in mid dash to the lobby doors before she disappeared.

Tenisha caught sight of the white muffler as it entered a vehicle down the block and drove off. She waved wildly to hail a taxi. "Follow that Pierce Arrow," she ordered the driver. "Faster, please. The light is changing!"

"He's heading into Harlem!" the driver exclaimed.

"I'll protect you," said his elegant-looking passenger. The driver's face flushed slightly. They flew down streets, uncrowded because of the hour. The streets were beginning to look familiar to Tenisha. Fifteen minutes later the Ford pulled up in front of 80 Edgecombe Avenue on Sugar Hill, the home of cosmetics heiress A'Lelia Walker. "Please wait. I won't be long." Tenisha hurried up the mansion steps. She was stopped at the door.

"I'm Miss Walker's niece. I was at her estate party last week, don't you remember?"

"Yes, I believe I do, but I don't recall your name on the list for tonight's celebration."

"I was unable to celebrate with everyone here, but I've just come from a personal meeting with the honoree herself, and someone who left The St. Regis just as I did dropped a paper that

I would like to return. I shouted to him, but he didn't hear me. His entrance here preceded mine by no more than two minutes."

"I'll return the paper to Mr. Davenport, Miss."

"It's rather personal. May I?" She pointed to the ballroom and the doorman stepped aside. Inside, Davenport, the muffler still at his neck, was laughing in camaraderie with a man as he put his arm around his wife's waist and turned her toward the ballroom entrance. It was midnight, early for some, but late for those with office hours in the morning, and several other couples were leaving too. Mrs. Davenport was accosted by a woman in a huge floral hat. Tenisha remembered her from the week before. She'd never stopped talking. Tenisha had precious minutes left before she encountered the Davenports and had to create lies at which she was totally inept and for which she was totally unprepared. Davenport had surely seen her with Ruth Elder. He would know he had been followed. She hurried to the foyer. She needed Aunt A'Lelia. The doorman had kept his eyes on her.

"He's busy; I won't disturb him. I'll telephone him in the morning. I must speak to my aunt. I'd appreciate your getting her for me."

"Yes, Miss. This way," and he escorted her to the parlor. Her aunt would not drop her guests to rush to speak to a niece who wasn't supposed to be there. She went into the parlor, where she could see the departing guests but not be seen by them. She hoped the taxi driver was still waiting. She saw the Davenports leave five minutes later, and ten minutes later Aunt A'Lelia bounced into the parlor.

"New developments in the murder?" she whispered, although they were quite alone.

"Maybe."

"Did George Davenport murder Lizette? Don't give me that look. I saw you at the ballroom door not more than a minute after he entered and, as you undoubtedly saw, I went to speak to him straightaway. Well?"

"I don't know. I saw him at Ruth Elder's hotel. She shouted a greeting to him that he should have heard. He ignored it and hurried away, so I followed him."

"He didn't want to meet her at all, or he would have come to my party for her. When I asked him why we wouldn't have the pleasure of his company this evening, he mumbled something about a meeting, and his protective wife said something like 'Poor darling, always working.'"

"Why do you say she's protective?"

"Last week I noticed that she always had an eye on him, even when she seemed engrossed in conversation, and if he was standing alone for more than a minute, she excused herself and hurried to him, taking his hand and leading him to someone to talk to before she fluttered off."

"Fluttered?"

"That feminine, coquetish thing that inherited wealth is so good at. Odd that he would have a meeting, and at such a late hour, at Ruth Elder's hotel."

"He could be a womanizer, first Lizette, who threatened to tell his wife if he dropped her or didn't pay her for her time, and now Ruth Elder, ready to cap all the adulation she's been getting with a romantic fling before flying home to Dullsville."

"The Lizette idea, maybe, but shouting a man's name through a hotel lobby doesn't imply a secret relationship."

"Very good, Auntie."

"Then, dear, don't I deserve some input from you on the case?"

"She didn't shout 'Davenport;' she shouted 'Coulet.'"

"A Frenchman! A mistake, perhaps."

"No, Auntie. She knew what she was seeing and what she was saying. George Davenport is Charles Coulet, President of La Belle Femme and Lizette's former employer."

"So, the handsome man at sea in a social setting is actually a man of at least two names and an accomplished actor!"

"Lily and I need to know more. Perhaps another meeting with more time to talk would give us enough information on which to build a respectable theory."

"Not here for at least six weeks; my social schedule is full. I could surprise them with passes to the Cotton Club and get you one too. Well, maybe not you. I don't like to ask for favors, even if the dancers do use my makeup."

"I'm not interested in seeing our people whooping and hollering like aborigines in skinny outfits anyway."

"I know, honey, but the Whites do the same thing in the Follies."

"Anyway, if I meet them too many times 'accidentally,' they may wonder why."

"You don't have to go; you have a White model working with you on the case."

"Yes, I could ask Lily, but who would introduce her to the Davenports? I don't think Mrs. Davenport would appreciate a stranger, who happens to be an attractive model, approaching her and her husband for a chat."

"It would probably be an extremely short chat. Familiar to them or not, you'd be a better choice. The Duke is trying to get the Club to lighten up on the rules so people of color can see their own kind making fools of themselves and making a bundle for the Club, but I can get you in, if you'd like."

"No, but thanks anyway, Auntie. At least you know what rules you'd be breaking. I wish I knew the murderer's rules."

"They're not set in cement, honey. They're set by fear. Fear sets the rules. Be careful."

"We don't see each other much anyway."

"True, but I'd still like to know that you exist."

"I'm glad to hear it, because I may not if you don't lend me taxi fare home. I'll return it next paycheck."

A'Lelia Walker put both hands on her hips. "How much money do you make?" She kissed her niece. "Repay me with news."

Chapter Twelve

Tenisha sat next to Lily in a corner of the staff lounge. "The boss is in overdrive this morning. There's already a huge demand for the dress Ruth Elder wore to the mayor's party for her. He anticipates the same for the other dresses she got here when he releases that information to the press."

"They're bound to ask about the fabrics, Ten, or he'll offer the information, as a courtesy to Walter Martin, if they don't. Since Singer and Martin are now linked, and since both have a relationship with La Belle Femme... I don't like this."

"Don't jump to frightening conclusions before you have to. Has Ted had a chance to find out anything?"

"He's in the air right now. He checked the books and saw that an order of fabrics was going to Iowa City, so he's flying them there personally. He told his dad it would impress the client. He's already made an appointment with Davenport about renting garage spaces in the event, highly unlikely, that Walter Martin Fabrics opens an office in Iowa City. He's missing his accounting class for a 'higher calling' --- helping me. His father is sure he's crazy and told him he's thinking of disowning him and adopting the receptionist, who'd inherit the business. She's studying accounting and actually shows up for the classes."

"Did you have a chance to look at the B. Altman ad I slipped you this morning?"

"Not yet." Lily removed the item from her dress pocket, unfolded the newsprint and read it aloud:

DRESSING YOUR TYPE

The 1st of 6 informal talks given by the editorial staff of VOGUE

Are you young, but plump? Your best lines will be brought out, your inches suppressed, in just the clothes you need. The tiny woman, the tailor-made type, the "arty lady," the girl of ice cream prettiness, the ugly but chic woman --- all will be shown what they should and shouldn't wear. Your problems will be solved --- beautifully, smartly, in every detail...

Questions are answered, if you have any left.

Living models --- smart clothes --- clever philosophy ---- and plenty of amusing action.

You are Cordially Invited.

"'Living models.' Poor Lizette. 'Ugly women.' Who wrote this ad?"

"I checked, Lee. It's the woman who funded the event --- Sheila Davenport."

"This is a no-nonsense, sharp-shooter, not likely to put up with a playboy husband. And an 'I will only marry for love' woman, who refused to marry handsome gold-diggers, is unlikely to be forgiving if the world finds out that with all her care she married badly. Oh, this is last week's ad. The fashion series starts today at three! Can you get Margaret to give you time off today?"

"Maybe, but Mrs. Davenport has seen me twice and you never."

"Bernie wouldn't let me out today for a Lilly Dache magazine ad. Miss Dache was kind enough to move it up to six o'clock. What possible reason can I give for leaving early?"

"Tell him that Mrs. Davenport will be using some of his clothes as demos for the event."

"He'll check and find out I was lying."

"He's not likely to check before you leave, and maybe she is using some of his clothes. He's unveiling his new collection at one of her charity events, so it would make sense for her to use some of his clothes today. Anyway, you don't have to say you know for sure that his clothes will be at B. Altman, just that you heard a rumor."

"I heard a rumor?"

"Yes, from me. I'm starting one right now. She'd be a fool not to have some Singers on display. When can you tell me all?"

"My place at eight? I can't bother dear, old Mr. Foster again. Every time I ask to use his telephone, I get a lecture on why an independent woman living alone should have one."

"Our conversation wouldn't interest him, anyway. I'm helping Donald study for an American history exam, so I may be a little late."

♦ ♦ ♦

Tenisha sighed deeply. Ah, blessed relief from those questions which, thank goodness, Donald had handled well. She sank into a chair and sipped her tea. "How did B. Altman's cure-all for the problem woman go?"

"Very well, if brow-beating the pliant woman into submission to the rules of fashion can be considered a success. I am happy to report that some of the living mannequins did indeed wear Bernard Singer creations. He can use that lucrative information in his ads. None of our clients was there, of course. Strictly wannabes. Showing up in a public forum in response to an ad like that would not appeal to them. The only chic women there sat with Sheila Davenport on stage to the right of the panel. The room was filled. I've never seen so many pads and pencils in an audience before. After each fashion harangue, women were invited to come to the stage for individual dissection for their own benefit and for the benefit of the not-so-brave cowering in their seats. I identified myself as a model from Bernard Singer Couture, thanked the Vogue panel for displaying some Singer creations, and asked several questions of the audience from a designer's point of view: What is the relative weight they would give to style versus comfort, which do they find more enticing, French or American fashions, and what is the favorite article of clothing in their closets? I also asked if they dress for themselves or for men."

"Well, you've certainly made this outing worth the loss of your time to Bernie. A summary of the results, please, Lee."

"Style edged out comfort, French was preferred over American and the closet favorite was a toss-up between the most comfortable and the most attention-getting garment. They all dress for themselves, if you can believe that!"

"I assume you got to talk personally to Sheila Davenport."

"Yes, I did. She's a woman of very definite ideas. She said that she knows she's not beautiful, but that clothes and character can make a woman appear so. She again expressed her gratitude to Bernie for his contribution of time, models and clothing to her charitable concern of the year --- abandoned girls. Then I asked her how she would respond to the questions I had asked the audience, and her response was rather amazing. She said that comfort was vastly preferable to style, but that stylish accessories would be sufficient to give a stylish illusion. She preferred American to French fashions because they were more, well, American, more suitable for American tastes and lifestyle, but that French touches could be added in bodice, belt or fabric to give a French fashion illusion. Her favorite article of clothing is an evening gown with billows of white chiffon intertwined with lace, cinched at the natural waist, with a U décolleté that stops just above the bustline. White ostrich feathers on the shoulders fan the air and undulate as she walks. It's worn with a black velvet cloche with black ostrich feathers standing tall and proud, and five-inch white ostrich leather pointed shoes. Her eyes actually glowed when she described this outfit. My mouth fell open, and all I could say was, 'It's a fairy tale ensemble! I've never seen you photographed in it.' She said, 'I've never worn it. It wouldn't suit me. And I dress for myself, which my husband prefers.' Then she excused herself to talk to a woman from the audience, who looked at her gray Chanel suit as if it were the epitome of designer elegance, which actually it was."

"The practical philanthropist is big on illusion."

"'I will only marry for love,' she said, remember? How disillusioned would a romanticist be if her husband disappointed her? Disillusioned enough to commission a murder? Or would her practical side take over with a more worldly and acceptable revenge?" Suddenly, there was an insistent knocking at the door.

"Who is it?" asked Lily.

"Open up!"

"Mr. Foster!" In her haste Lily fumbled with the lock. Standing before her was an elderly man with brown hair falling over his forehead and his hands on his hips.

"Just what are you doing!" He shuffled into the room. "This letter was shoved under my door. I thought it was from you, but it was for you. I opened it because there was no return address on the envelope, and I was suspicious. You're in trouble, my girl! You're paid to be a model, so stop playing vigilante before you give me a stroke!" He pulled a handkerchief from his pocket to mop his brow, as Lily and Tenisha edged him over to the wingback chair. He plopped into it with relief. Lily took the envelope he was still clutching, opened it, unfolded the letter and read:

If you wish to remain alive, I suggest that you stop interfering in police business. One dead model is more than enough. Anyone assisting you will regret it. You will discover too late that the force aligned against you cannot allow you to succeed. This is a serious warning and well meant.

Tenisha took it from her hand and read it to herself. "It's unsigned, of course, and you can't trace a letter typed on dime store stationery."

"Maybe we can." Lily turned to Mr. Foster. "You sell typewriters. What brand typed this?"

"You must report this to the police!"

"I will, I will, but the typewriter..."

"It's a Royal."

"And the paper?"

He held it up to the light of the wrought iron chandelier. "It's hard to tell. Many offices use this texture and weight."

"So, you think it's office stationery."

"Probably, the typewriter is. Look, are you calling the police or not?"

"Yes, of course, but since only one person in this room has immediate access to a telephone..."

"Fine, I'll call them." Mr. Foster shuffled to the door.

"If we need your advice on the ribbon that typed---"

Mr. Foster's glare silenced Lily.

"Of course, the police. Thank you, Mr. Foster," said Tenisha.

"The ribbon that typed this will have the imprint of the words in this letter, but I suppose scouring every office typewriter in the city isn't an option, and the typist may already have changed the ribbon."

"I suppose. 'A serious warning well meant' doesn't sound like it's written by a violent person, Lee, but it's out of our hands now, and good riddance to it, I say."

Lily answered a triple knock on the door.

"You should ask who it is before you answer the door. Your boyfriend's on the telephone."

"Thanks, Pete, I'll be right there. Will you walk me to the luncheonette, Ten?"

"Of course. A woman living alone who opens doors willy, nilly and receives a threatening letter shouldn't be allowed out alone."

◆ ◆ ◆

"Oh, Ted! Where are you?"

"I'm in a single room in some dump. Listen, I just spoke to Ira Compton, our client. I brought a sampling of our latest fabrics too, and he loves them. Since Davenport did buy fabrics for Lizette, and since Tenisha thought he had some knowledge of fashion, on a hunch I showed Compton a picture of Davenport. He recognized him! He said he was Jonathan Bennett, a former intern at Compton and a graduate of the Iowa School of Design. He's an excellent draftsman and a creative fabric designer. In fact, some of the fabric designs Dad developed were inspired by Bennett's designs! Compton asked if Bennett was working with us, and I said we did transact some business for him. He asked me to give Jonathan his best wishes and said that the School of Design has never sent him a better student."

"Did you show him a picture of Lizette?"

"Yes, and of Dupre, too, but he didn't know them."

"Well done, Ted. Are you coming home, now?"

"Of course not. I have an appointment tomorrow morning with the dean at the School of Design. I want more information about Bennett, and I have an afternoon appointment with Arthur Davenport about those bogus garage-space rentals. Let's find out what he knows."

"Ted, you are a detective diamond in the rough, and not so rough! You know, you will have missed two accounting classes."

"Yeah, well... I'll make them up."

"Maybe Tenisha can help you. She does wonders helping her boyfriend prepare for exams."

Tenisha began a loud protest, and Lily quickly said, "Thank you, darling. See you soon."

Ted replaced the receiver, a look of wonder on his face. Lily had never called him "darling" before.

"You didn't tell him that you got that letter or that we're off the case."

"He was so excited, I just couldn't. He wasn't meant to be an accountant. He was meant to be a dashing, young man-about-town and a husband."

"Occupations that don't pay the bills, or is he expecting his wife to pay them."

"Of course not, Ten." She sighed. "Meanwhile he's found something he can do, and do well. I won't spoil it for him."

"Don't forget, he's part of 'anyone assisting you will regret it' --- and so am I!"

"We'll let the professionals solve the murder, but it is our civic duty to help if we can, answering questions about what we know. It's a crime to withhold evidence."

"Tell that to the writer of the letter. Oh, dear, Aunt A'Lelia is tangentially involved. I hope the letter writer and the murderer, if they're different, ignore tangents. Auntie does not want to regret anything."

Lily saw Ten off on the bus and walked slowly back to her small, cozy apartment. She thought of Bennett/Davenport/Coulet, whose secret passion was designing fabrics and fashions, and of her passion, becoming an opera singer. It wasn't a secret, but it was stalled. Singing Singer's dresses onto the runway was not an entrée to the Metropolitan Opera. It would not stun on a resume. She would check the newspaper for operas the Met was performing. Ted would take her soon to keep the dream going, and to fade, at least a little, the sad and dangerous events of late. She stood for a moment under the gas lamp at the corner, admiring how the light made a dent in the darkness in all directions. Spirits were lifted a touch, even in semi-darkness. Music could do that too, and so could clothing. Music and fashion ensembles could make you feel better about yourself and your world which, oddly enough, was what she currently was doing for others. Her turn would come if she were patient -- and if she stayed alive.

♦ ♦ ♦

Lily would have waited for the sun to pour through her window, but she had to get to work earlier today. Bernard Singer was unveiling, in utmost secrecy, the spring collection he would be premiering at Mrs. Davenport's charity event. His models appreciated this early peek at the clothes, and he appreciated seeing how they looked on them. Lily had heard that last season some items had been modeled by all the girls so that the boss could determine which "type" it looked best on. Then he had made adjustments so that it looked good on all of them. A scarf here, belt there could make the difference. Lily remembered what Mrs. Davenport had said about accessories. And a Simplicity Pattern of a Singer original, even in a lesser fabric, could make women of modest income stylish. Singer's adjustments were always made with the idea of translating them into Simplicity Patterns. Bernard Singer believed that every woman was entitled to enjoy the limelight.

Mrs. Davenport was there promptly at nine, and Mr. Singer greeted her warmly. He introduced the models she would shortly see displaying the gowns for the event. The Singer touch was always humane and personal, with his staff as well as his clients. Tenisha, sitting to a side, but well within earshot of the pair, served as secretary, taking notes about comments and responses. Yes, he would display splashes of color without ignoring the more somber, more "realistic," as she put it, tones in suits and dresses. He recommended opening with a totally feminine, girlish, daring look, which he would then demonstrate how to adapt to women of all types. The showing went well, and even Margaret, of stiff upper lip and clothes, allowed the office staff, as well as herself, to witness the rehearsal. All were well aware that a word to an outsider about what they had seen meant instant dismissal. Tenisha's shorthand was equal to her task as, for two hours, the models paraded and adjustments in order, commentary, and music were made. At last, Singer thanked the models and walked Mrs. Davenport to the elevator. All were allowed two hours for lunch until one o'clock, when there would be a showing of suits for Mr. Dawson, who wanted to surprise his wife with something smart for her birthday.

Though the models and staff chatted in the elevator, Tenisha and Lily were silent until they reached the street and headed for a dinner spot that would be open but empty at lunchtime. Seated at a corner table, Tenisha pulled out her notepad and placed it in front of Lily, whose shorthand was almost as good as hers. Lily read:

"We could easily incorporate the clothes into a Parisian theme, with Montmartre, the Eiffel Tower, Parc Vendome creating backgrounds for the ensembles. Perhaps your husband could appear on stage, a masculine touch, nodding his approval of the clothes."

"People will think we're advertising our newest travel bureau in Paris. I couldn't bear to have them believe we're using a charity event for personal gain. And while my handsome husband's appearance might appeal to the ladies, it does not appeal to me. Anyway, Paris is far from his mind; I wish it weren't. He insists that one of our French executives open the new shop, ribbon-cutting and all, and all is going to be a lot: quiche, balloons, desserts. He's un-persuadable. Photos of the president of Wainwright Travel in Paris would be an asset in our advertising."

"But I've seen photos of him in Spain, Italy, Germany..."

"Yes, indeed, but he won't go to Paris."

"Ruth Elder met him in Paris as Coulet. He can't appear there as anyone else. How many identities does the man have? Maybe your Ted can discover who he really is."

"I thought the police were going to do that, Ten."

"Yes, well..." The waiter had just taken their order, and they were about to relax with a Tom Collins and a gin and tonic when two men entered the nearly empty restaurant. They were Davenport and Dupre, and there was no place to hide.

Chapter Thirteen

"I appreciate your time, Dean Arnold. I delivered some of my father's fabrics to Ira Compton yesterday, and he was raving about the talents of one of his former interns who was one of your former students, Jonathan Bennett. Dad is interested in adding more talent to the company's design team, and I'd be grateful if you could give me more information about Mr. Bennett."

"It's been ten years since his graduation, but he's hard to forget. He could design a dish towel that would make you want to wash dishes all day. Every form of women's clothing and household fabric were a breeze for his creative mind, but his creativity worked in sync with practicality, so that the clothes, bed sheets, sofa covers were comfortable, like a second skin. He assembled dozens of scrapbooks in his "History of Design" class. He didn't need them for the class, he wanted them for himself. His special interest was women's clothing. He had pictures of the current designs from all the big European and American houses. It frustrated him that he could not see ahead to what they would be in six months, so that he could emulate them, adapt them, or better yet, outdo them with designs of his own. He was a very ambitious young man."

"Do you know how I could contact him?"

"It's been ten years, as I said, and a lot can happen in that time. When he graduated, he said that he was going to New York to apprentice in a design house. He always thought big town and big time. He'd won two thousand dollars in our Seniors Design Contest, and he said that would do for room and board until he got a design position. He left for New York loaded with recommendations from the faculty and Ira Compton, promising to keep us apprised of his progress, but we never heard from him. Iowa is worlds away from New York, not just geographically, and possibly our school, its faculty and the designers in our area count as nothing in New York. His talents should have vastly overridden any doubts the New York houses might have had about his design background, but such is not always the case."

"Perhaps he's on a design staff, but ashamed to tell you he's not a star."

"It's possible."

"Surely his family would know his whereabouts."

"His mother died when he was six, no siblings, just a father, if you can call the man who sired him and disowned him a father. Jonathan came to us on scholarship and remained on scholarship throughout his time here, living in our dormitory. He had worked during high school as an automotive mechanic and continued nights when he came here. That was his father's dream for him, to have his own automotive repair service, something the father was never able to achieve."

"His father might know what's become of him."

"Not likely, and no, I do not have an address for that horrid man." Dean Arnold looked at his watch. "Is there anything else, Mr. Martin?"

Ted Martin flagged a taxi and was about to say 145 Oak Street. Instead, he said, "Take me to the nearest automotive repair service. When they arrived, he said "Please wait." He hurried in, impatiently waited behind a customer describing in vivid detail the miracle he expected the mechanic to produce on his five-year-old Ford, and finally was able to ask, "Sir, do you know a mechanic named Bennett?" He repeated this several times, the taxi driver glancing often and happily at the meter. Ted Martin finally said, "145 Oak Street."

Arthur Davenport was a thin, pinch-nosed man who greeted Ted Martin graciously. He detailed the virtues of each of his six garages in the area, explaining which locations were in proximity to areas conducive to a design firm. The cost would depend on the number of spaces he would need for staff and clients. Mr. Martin must realize that on-street parking would be minimal in the desirable central locations. The young man took copious notes, but not to be outdone, Davenport produced a sheaf of carefully typed facts and figures for him to forward to his father. Ted Martin thought he had done a creditable job of wasting his time. Asking Arthur Davenport about the bogus George Davenport was pointless, or was it?

"Mr. Davenport, if our vehicles should need servicing..."

"Oh, didn't I mention that? We have an excellent staff of mechanics, supervised by the best of his kind in the city."

"Jonathan Bennett?"

"No, no, though I believe he has a son of that name. Douglas Bennett can cure any automotive ailment. Of course, he doesn't often do it himself; he supervises a staff that does most of the hands-on work, but our clients appreciate that a man of his mechanical caliber is available to them when emergencies arise. He visits all our garages daily and is, I believe, one of the chief reasons Davenport Garages is patronized by the highest-ranking officials in the city."

"You're not afraid that your competition will spirit him away?"

"We pay well, Mr. Martin, and the honor of working for us and being in close proximity to the most respected and influential leaders in our community cannot be duplicated."

"Would you object to my speaking to Mr. Bennett?"

"Not at all, only he returns tonight from a vacation and won't be available for an interview until tomorrow afternoon. After two weeks in Las Vegas, it may take him yet another day or two to decompress and re-acclimate from a lavish hotel suite to his modest apartment near the park. It's more than our generous salary that allows him to vacation this way. Bennett's always been a saver, and two years ago he decided to live a dream life, on vacation at least. Otherwise, the man's a realist."

"Would you arrange a meeting for me?"

"I'll write you a letter of introduction and give you his telephone number. You can arrange a meeting at your mutual convenience."

Ted knew that there was no convenience for a man who was already two days overdue at work.

Chapter Fourteen

Dupre and Davenport waved to Lily and Tenisha and were seated at an opposite corner of the dining room. They spoke briefly before Dupre walked to their table and invited them to dine with him and his friend. Drinks in hand, they made their way past empty tables to do just that.

"Miss Chasen, this is Mr. Davenport. Miss Jones, you two have met before, of course, and I, Miss Jones, am Charles Dupre, you both have undoubtedly enjoyed your private viewing," he nodded to Tenisha, "and participation," he nodded to Lily, "in the rehearsal of the clothes to be shown at Mrs. Davenport's benefit in January. You are here, no doubt, to have lunch and to view through the prism of your intellects another private matter, having to do with us."

"For a friend you recently didn't know and whom you suspected of murdering your common-law wife, you have provided us with luncheon conversation," said Lily.

"As you can see, we do know each other and are willing to satisfy your curiosity about our relationship triangle if you promise to remain silent and not share what we say with the police. What we will tell you has nothing to do with the murder of Lizette, but we do wish to put your minds at ease."

"And not create needless trouble," added Lily.

"Precisely. I did harbor some suspicion of my friend, and I hoped that with his wife's upcoming charity event, courtesy of Bernard Singer Couture, and your involvement with Walter Martin, both past and present, in the form of his son, you might be able to put my mind at ease about George."

"You don't mean discover the truth about any personal involvement he had with Lizette?"

"Both. I was hoping that the truth would satisfy me. There's a lot riding on our relationship."

"We're business partners," said George, "and Lizette, in addition to being Charles' lover, was the intermediary for our design firm."

"La Belle Femme, Mr. Coulet?"

George Davenport smiled slightly. "Yes, Miss Chasen. Our dreams ride on its success."

Lily thought of Sheila Davenport's dreams of being feminine and alluring, of looking regal and smashing in clothes, of being wanted, loved, adored for herself, not for her money.

"We all have dreams," said Tenisha, her mind flitting briefly to the image of John Robert Powers. "With your wealth why must a fashion house be secret? Surely your wife would not object to it."

"A leading question, Miss Jones, and one to which I read in your face that you know the answer. My wealth consists only of my income, my opulent income from being President of Wainwright Travel. Our prenuptial agreement bars me from receiving any of my wife's inheritance. She didn't think I needed it anyway; Davenport Garages in Iowa gave me enough of a cushion of wealth should our marriage, somehow, fall apart.

However, Davenport Garages is not the gold mine she imagines it to be."

"Not for you, anyway, Mr. Bennett."

George Davenport looked at Lily intently. "What more do you know about me?"

"Only that you worked your way through Iowa School of Design as an auto mechanic, were thought the world of by the faculty and by Ira Compton, for whom you interned, that you came to New York to make your mark in the world of women's design and married into a travel agency. Your years here between your arrival and your marriage are a blank. Would you care to enlighten me?"

On George Davenport's face was renewed respect for the pretty model. "The fashion world totally ignored me. I fell back on my knowledge of auto mechanics. It provided the basics, room and board and the money to fund the appearance of wealth, to look the part of who I wanted to be, rather than who I was, a poor man who had no right to hobnob with the wealthy or dream of being one of them through talent alone."

"You met your wife through a party given by some visiting duke or earl. How were you able to get yourself invited to that?"

"I wasn't invited. I attended in my usual manner; I crashed. I crashed so often in my handsome clothes, that people hailed me in recognition and thought I belonged. I was to them a playboy who had run away from a life of garages, but still enjoyed the advantages of wealth. No one even thought to question that lie. After a while I began to believe it myself!"

"Surely your wife would have funded your design ambitions. Why keep secret the existence of La Belle Femme?"

"Because, Miss Chasen, it would be an admission of my poverty. She might think I had married her for her money. This would hardly have been an auspicious beginning to our marriage. Indeed, there might have been no marriage at all."

Tenisha stared at George Davenport as he spoke. "Did you marry her for her money?"

"The niceties, the decorum of conversation seems to escape you, Miss Jones."

"Social pleasantries have no place in a discussion of events that culminate in murder."

"So true, Miss Jones. What was I thinking?"

"That you needed time to formulate an answer to my question."

"I admire and respect my wonderful wife. She acts on her love and faith in people, and her generosity and kindness are bywords in a social set that too often considers self the ultimate concern in life."

"But did you marry her for her money?" Tenisha persisted.

"I married her for the person she is, and I am honored to be her husband."

"What about your relationship with Lizette? Was it solely a business one?" asked Lily.

"Nothing is solely anything, Miss Chasen. There are many elements to a relationship. Ours was primarily business. She may have imagined a more personal interest on my part, but women, over time, do tend to imagine such things, present company excepted, I am sure."

Don't be so sure, thought Lily, and don't think such imaginings apply only to one sex.

Charles noted the expression on Lily's face and nodded agreement with her thoughts. "Men may gaze at attractive women as women may at men. We may go beyond gazing as well, but this does not erase a commitment of the heart, that is what is important. We French may not enter into legal commitments for this very reason."

"Our business arrangement was paramount," cut in Davenport. "

"All else was secondary and of passing interest."

"Well, Mr. Bennett-Davenport-Coulet, you've made that quite clear." Anger began to work on Davenport's face. "But you are a charming man, which makes your ambition easier to accept." Davenport's eyes locked on Tenisha's, but the flush began to subside.

Lily leaned toward the men. "Then if Lizette's behavior was not a serious issue with either of you, and you were, like us, aghast at her murder, why do you think she was eliminated?"

"Eliminated?" echoed Charles Dupre.

"Yes," continued Lily, "as paid intermediary, possible informant concerning your secret activities, potential partner."

"There was never a chance that she would become a partner, and never any indication that this would interest her. And she was more than an employee. There was no reason to destroy such a lovely creature, so vital, so full of life...." Charles Dupre could not go on.

"I understand, and my heart cries with you. I enjoyed her company so much."

"I know. There was a kindness between you. But the other models were cruel --- ignoring her, imitating her, laughing at her. Yet the police can find none of them to charge with her murder."

"Charles, why did she come to Bernard Singer Couture?"

"Our star is rising in Parisian couture, Miss Chasen, and we wanted to link with a rising star in American couture. We suggested Lizette, and Mr. Singer realized the opportunity for both our houses."

"Lizette could have sung our clothes onstage, but Mr. Singer was not aware she could sing. Both Francois and Lizette singing would have made our presentations even more unique."

"Singing models are harder to replace, and Lizette's work at Singer was meant to be temporary. My poor darling was a needless victim, perhaps to prevent our fashion union."

"How could eliminating a model do that? My death might be lamented at Singer, but it would not affect the success of the firm." Both men were silent.

"Is Charles Dupre your real name?" asked Tenisha.

"Yes, of course."

"You are a man of one name, a known background in accounting and no secrets to upset your family or the public?"

"My father is upset. I was to succeed him in his accounting firm, but no, no secrets."

"Creativity coupled with accounting pleases you more."

"Much more."

Tenisha turned toward George Davenport. "But you, Mr. Davenport, are a man of three names, with secrets. Could at least one of them have disturbed someone enough to lead to Lizette's murder?"

"Possibly, but if you're thinking that a jealous wife wanted to destroy her competition, that's nonsense. My wife knows where I am at all times."

"Including now?"

"Yes. She knows I'm with a male business associate."

"In your travel firm."

"A male business associate. Period. It's the truth."

"As far as it goes, it certainly is."

"When I'm not at work my wife and I are inseparable."

"Is that natural behavior for a couple? Is that healthy?"

"It is for us to decide what's natural and healthy in our relationship, Miss Jones! My wife is not a murderer, so put that out of your mind!"

Tenisha shot a quick glance at Lily. Yes, it was best to put out of one's mind the thought that a meal ticket, far beyond hamburger, and the pockets whose contents kept La Belle

Femme liquid could possibly be a murderer. Tenisha recalled her meeting with Sheila Davenport at her aunt's party and Lily's meeting with her at B. Altman.

"Do you expect to reveal your fashion activities to your wife?"

"At the right moment. Is that all, Miss Jones?"

Lily stood up. "Mr. Dupre, Mr. Davenport, we've intruded enough on your business meeting with a painful subject that is beyond our ability to decipher. We will keep our word and not reveal this conversation to anyone before you gentlemen do, if ever you do. So, thank you for inviting us over. We will now leave you to your lunch."

"'At the right moment,'" repeated Tenisha as they returned to their table. "Is there ever a right moment to tell your wife that you've been lying to her, that your background is not what she thinks it is, that you're using your income --- hopefully he hasn't raided the cash register --- to promote a business about which she thinks you know nothing, that you respect but do not love her?"

"She knows he doesn't love her. A wife who attempts to watch her husband's every move, who's proud of his looks, but afraid to have other women look at him too long, who still keeps a dream ensemble in her closet --- she knows."

"As long as she doesn't admit it to herself, she's safe."

"The truth tends to find a way to emerge. I hope that applies to the murderer, and soon!"

Tenisha looked at their empty glasses. "We need something stronger." She hailed the waiter. As they sliced the beef and forked the carrots, two men entered the restaurant. They looked at the women and then at the men before walking to the men's table. They were Inspector Kirk and his assistant. They sat for five minutes with the men before rising and walking toward the women.

"Are you ladies all right?"

"Yes, thank you. We were here first," blurted Lily.

"Do you think they were following you, Miss Chasen?"

"I don't know. I hope not."

"They didn't speak to you?"

"They waved."

"I see. Would you like my man to follow you back to work after you've finished here?"

"Oh, no, please. If they're not suspicious of us, we wouldn't want to give them cause to be. Both do business with Singer."

"I understand, but if you feel the need for police services, do let me know." He tipped his hat and left, his man following.

"If I were a policeman," said Tenisha, "I'd think it strange that two sets of suspects appear, even at a distance, at the same time in an empty restaurant."

"Then it's a good thing that you're not a policeman."

Chapter Fifteen

As the elevator opened on the second floor, Lily's jaw dropped. "Mr. Martin!" Walter Martin blocked her way, waited until Tenisha, after a quick glance at him, had entered Singer Couture and the hall was empty, before clearing his throat and addressing the stunned model.

"Miss Chasen, I realize you have a one o'clock fitting, but Mr. Singer has kindly allowed me to delay you for a few minutes of conversation." He escorted her into Singer Couture and directly to Singer's office. He knocked, Bernard Singer opened the door and with a nod to them both abandoned his office. Walter Martin sat on the sofa, pointing Lily to the facing chair.

"I trust your discretion as a valued model at this house. I must tell you I am worried. Inspector Kirk thinks I should have personally dealt with Lizette Frere when she came to our establishment, as if a CEO and chief fabric designer meets all his customers. We didn't craft original designs for her; she bought from our seasonal designs for the public. And now, with Charles Dupre, her lover and boss, requesting us to craft designs for the exclusive use of La Belle Femme, the truth seems to make me out a liar. It's beyond the inspector's cerebral power to understand that a customer can admire your usual fare to such a degree that he might commission unusual fare, original designs to grace HIS clothes, to enhance them, to call attention to THEIR originality and charm. Since all that I've heard is hearsay and unreliable, I must ask you whether Charles Dupre and Lizette Frere seemed devoted to each other and whether George Davenport, if he ever appeared to retrieve the fabrics for her, seemed to regard her in an intimate way. I ask this because his wife's occasional patronage at our house, and hopefully continued patronage after the charity gala Bernard is hosting, affects the future of our firm. Bernie expects his use of our fabrics, created specifically to his designs, to escalate. A love triangle is ticklish business and can be devastating to innocent professionals caught in the middle."

"I understand your concern, Mr. Martin, but we live in an era when sensationalism is appreciated and rewarded."

"Not by my clientele! If Bernie and I must devise plans to mitigate any disastrous fallout from the situation, we must have input from someone more knowledgeable about the parties involved. You can't deny that you knew Miss Frere better than anyone at this house, that you met George and Sheila Davenport at one of A'Lelia Walker's parties, and that you had a personal conversation with Mrs. Davenport at the first Vogue panel event at B. Altman."

"I did not meet the Davenports at Miss Walker's party. Her niece, Tenisha Jones, our assistant office manager, did."

Walter Martin jumped to his feet and paced the office. "Too many people involved, too many people to question. The only frustrations I should have should relate to running my firm." He ran his hands through his hair and sat down.

"Mr. Martin, I did, on another occasion, meet Mr. Davenport, and I clearly sensed that he had no intention of creating a barrier between himself and his wife. They have an odd, but strong, relationship. They need each other. Mr. Dupre and Mr. Davenport are aware of each other's existence and respect each other. They have a relationship beyond Lizette."

"Of course! Wainwright Travel's new location in Paris! Uniforms for the staff, perhaps, and possibly Singer models in their ads."

"Possibly. Forgive an intrusive question, but how long have you been supplying our house with fabrics?"

"Two years. We were introduced by a part-time agent from one of Bernie's previous suppliers. He anticipated being sacked, and thought a good deed might insure future employment. As it turned out he was promoted, but my ideas and Bernie's meshed, and a good relationship developed."

"Was this agent with a New York supplier?"

"No, he was from somewhere out West. Bernie met him at a convention here."

"Do you recall his name?"

"Jonathan Bennett."

Lily was taken aback. "And his appearance?"

"Very tall, with a thick moustache and a goatee. An intellectual type, rather a fish out of water, here. Do you know him?"

"Only by reputation."

"Then he was successful. I'm glad! Walter Martin going international. I never dreamed that big!"

Dreams again!

"I won't trouble you further, Miss Chasen. It was kind of you to speak to a man who fired you, which, I must admit, may have been a mistake. If you were still with us, my son would not have made that needless trip to Iowa. The distraction of your presence would at least have kept him at home. He would be here, working, studying. Heaven knows what's keeping him there. A woman's influence can be dramatic, galvanizing a man to do what is best for himself, his father, his firm. Yes, I may have misjudged you, Miss Chasen. If so, I regret it."

Never one to apologize easily, Walter Martin had addressed the carpet. He now looked Lily Chasen in the eyes. His began to mist, and she reached for the hand he offered. She sighed. Poor man, she thought, with no one to console and guide him, and he was rightly distraught about his company's future and his son. He had not misjudged her at all.

Lily was in mid-fitting when Tenisha dropped by to convey Mr. Singer's appreciation for her agreeing to talk to Mr. Martin. As the seamstress moved off to retrieve more pins, Tenisha moved closer to the tall figure on the pedestal. "Martin had a talk with me about my impression of Davenport at auntie's party. He doesn't appreciate the economic value of scandal."

"That's just what I told him."

♦ ♦ ♦

On her way home, Lily stopped by the corner luncheonette. "Any messages, Tony?"

"Your boyfriend called and said be here tomorrow morning before you catch the bus to work. He'll telephone at 8:30."

"Thanks, Tony."

"I feel like a third wheel in your love life. Why don't you ---"

"I know, 'get a telephone, '" she chorused with him.

Chapter Sixteen

Lily almost missed her stop on the bus, as she thought about what Ted had told her. The president of Davenport Garages was, as the library photo had revealed, not the Davenport who now led his wife's travel empire. His father, Douglas Bennett, was Davenport's chief automotive mechanic. But Bennett had struck Ted as odd. He had spoken in detail and with relish about his work, but he was firm and unwavering in all that he said, whether it was about automobiles, politics or social mores. His beliefs were clearly defined, there were no shades of gray and he had "a glass laugh." When he was asked about his son his words were sharp and clear, when he spoke of automotive abilities his eyes shone, when the subject turned to fashion design his eyes hooded over, and his remarks were severe and unforgiving. Lily recalled a similar severity by the son in the restaurant, but he was being challenged to defend the basis of his marriage. His father was not defending a choice, nor was his honor at stake. Ted said that the father believed that the son's career was a given that the son refused to accept. Douglas Bennett seemed to think in absolutes. Behavior was either right or wrong. He did not allow that the young man's choice could be different from what he had envisioned as his son's destiny. Ted said that "he laughed a lot without any humor and smiled a lot without any pleasure." Lily alighted from the bus, pressed the collar of her coat closer to her neck to ward off the nippy morning breeze and walked quickly the two blocks to work. Perhaps the son took after the mother. Perhaps the passing of the mother had never been fully processed or accepted by the husband, or perhaps Lily was being generous in excusing the behavior of a deficient father. It was hard to imagine why such a stiff man would go on holiday to Las Vegas, as apparently he often did. As for his current relationship with his son, Ted said that he had affirmed closure in their association. Jonathan Bennett had dishonored his work heritage. He had chosen a "soft" job when he entered the design field, and had only aborted that occupation to enter a still softer job as an office mannequin for a travel company he hadn't even established. He had married into a ready-made occupation as the pretty-boy husband of a wealthy heiress. The son he had raised no longer existed. He had been replaced by an inferior mutation. A question about whether he had attended his son's wedding two years earlier met with stony silence. Ted must have looked puzzled, because Bennett followed this with an emphatic "No!" Lily recalled the news reports that said Bennett/Davenport only had New York friends in attendance, that his brother was in Australia and that his parents were long dead. The real Davenport brother had indeed been in Australia at the time. No one had questioned this story told by the charming, dashing young man who freely spent what was presumed to be his "garages" inheritance.

♦ ♦ ♦

The lobby was busy, the usual start to a workday. Lily saw with dismay that Inspector Kirk, leaning against a pillar, had started to walk toward her. He motioned at a sofa and they sat down.

"I must sign in, Inspector. May we do this at another time?"

"I won't keep you. Just one minute of your time, please. Have you noticed someone following you?"

"Your men, Inspector, but I've tuned them out and gone about my business."

"Besides my men, Miss Chasen."

"No, have others been following me?"

"Yes, we were following you first, of course, but we were about to discontinue it when we noticed that someone else was doing the same. Since women are in and out of this establishment all day, and since the neighborhood is replete with women and men engaged in fashion work of one kind or another, it's not unusual to see the same faces in the street, but my men noticed that one woman, nicely and variously dressed, was following you. When you waited to cross a street, she stopped and waited a short distance behind you. When you went into a luncheonette for a Danish and coffee, she waited outside, thumbing through magazines at a newsstand until you reappeared and she continued walking behind you."

"Why would someone be following me?"

"We determined to find out, so when you returned to your apartment, my men followed her. Last night I went with them, gained entrance to her apartment and spoke to her."

"What did she want of me?"

"She's employed by a private detective agency, and she was instructed to find out who were your male acquaintances, and at what hours you saw them and what activities you engaged in."

"That would be impossible once I was indoors, especially in the privacy of my apartment."

"There are ways to invade privacy, shadows on window shades and the like. She complained that with no telephone to tap you made her job more difficult."

"Thank heavens for that! Who would employ someone to do such a thing and why?"

"A woman who feared that her husband and Lizette Frere were having an affair and that perhaps she wasn't the only one."

"Sheila Davenport."

"Yes, and I am asking your permission to have her arrested for stalking you."

"Mr. Singer is doing a benefit for her that can bring him priceless publicity. Ruth Elder started the social avalanche and linked him to Parisian couture, and Mrs. Davenport can keep those benefits flowing."

"We may be close to solving the murder of Lizette Frere, your friend and co-worker, and you must see how putting this case to rest vastly outweighs in importance to society the publicity for a fashion house. Without an official charge against Mrs. Davenport, we cannot detain her. This is a MURDER case, Miss Chasen, not a society bazaar. I am asking you, pleading with you to file a charge against Mrs. Davenport. Will you do that?"

"Absolutely not!"

Chapter Seventeen

Lily looked up at the white limestone building on Park Avenue. The crenelated towers above the Davenport penthouse caught the rays of a blazing sun. The doorman ushered her in. She announced her presence and, after a quick check, was escorted to the elevator, whose attendant soon bowed her out. Was this what it meant to be rich? she thought. To be overtly, showily rich, to be sure. She wondered if George Davenport had completely acclimated to it. Mrs. Davenport waited at the door to her apartment and greeted her.

"No, I don't usually open our entry door," she answered, assuming the question which was on Lily's lips, though it wasn't. "The staff is off, which is why I insisted on an appointment today, and I had charitable business to conduct before this hour and will have two hours hence, which is why I said I would see you at this time."

"Do you always explain appointments this way?"

"Often. This way there can be no misunderstanding about when to be in a given place, who invited whom, and the purpose of the meeting. I have omitted the last because you did not state your purpose. I usually do not agree to a meeting without a stated purpose."

"Then I appreciate your agreeing to this one. No, no beverage of any kind, thank you."

"Well, then?" Mrs. Davenport sat back, expectant.

"For the past two weeks you have had me followed. Why?"

"She wasn't very good at it if you noticed."

"I didn't notice. Detective Inspector Kirk noticed and informed me of it. His men, watching me, became aware they were not alone in this activity. The woman had no choice but to admit that she was in your employ. I ask again, why?"

"Since you are employed at the firm where the unfortunate model died, and were previously employed at the firm at which she bought fabric for her clothes, I was curious about your after-hour associations. Singer Couture is most kindly hosting our benefit, but any more than a passing involvement in the model's murder would not cast the charity, or me, in a favorable light. It's not a matter of pride or egotism, Miss Chasen, merely a logical consideration to assure that the reputation of the charities I sponsor are not sullied, as they might be, if my associations were called into question."

"Were you put at ease by the woman's conclusions?"

"I must say I was. I hope now that your mind is likewise put at ease over this surveillance."

"Actually, it is not, Mrs. Davenport. While you were concerned about my connection to a murder, I am concerned about your connection to it, and Inspector Kirk is, too."

"That's nonsense! What has Lizette Frere got to do with me?"

"That's what we'd like to know, and what you would like to know, too. You watch your husband like a hawk, but---"

"That's quite enough! How dare you impugn the happiness of my marriage. It is all goodness and light, just as it appears to be. I answered your initial question. No more questions are warranted or welcome. Good day, Miss Chasen!"

"Would you rather speak to Inspector Kirk? He wanted you arrested for having me stalked so that he could question you more closely on circumstances surrounding Miss Frere's murder. Wouldn't you rather speak to a young model, whose actual goal is to become an opera singer, than to an experienced policeman, whose goal is the apprehension and execution of the murderer of Lizette Frere?"

"The arrest for stalking—"

"I refused him. How long have you had detectives following your husband? I shan't repeat it to him, I promise."

"What makes you think I've done any such thing?"

"Come, now, Mrs. Davenport."

"Since I noticed modest but unusual expenses in his accounts. I do believe in privacy, Miss Chasen, but our marriage is still a young one, and good management of the company my father built is a sacred trust to me. George had done it very well, but I noticed modest, but unspecified expenditures in the business accounts. I didn't find them alarming, but I am a cautious person."

"Did you attempt to discover where the monies went?"

"Yes, on occasion I've had clothes made to order, purchasing fabrics at Walter Martin. The expenditures seemed similar to the way Mr. Martin prices his fabrics, but when I asked him about the possibility that my husband was buying me fabrics to surprise me, he said that the only obviously gift fabrics he sold during that time frame were to a Mr. Smith for a Miss Lizette Frere, who, according to his records, picked them up in person. Before our marriage George had an eye for the ladies and they for him, but since our marriage he has been completely devoted to me."

"And you to him, to the extent of watching him carefully."

"I have a faithful husband, Miss Chasen, but men are men. I know that I am not a raving beauty, and with the passage of time in a marriage..."

"Two years?"

"Is there anything else you care to know to put the inspector's mind and yours at ease?"

"Did you consider me a threat?

"Certainly not. I was merely taking the kind of precaution even a beautiful woman would consider, and the results proved that the trust I have in my husband is fully justified."

"Then you did not murder Lizette Frere? I ask as Inspector Kirk's proxy."

"I certainly did not!"

"Thank you, Mrs. Davenport. I know this cannot have been an easy interview for you. Oh, by the way, did you discover what the unusual business expenditure was for?"

"I assumed it was related to the Parisian travel bureau we were then planning, and which is now about to open. The checks went to Paris."

Lily headed for the door behind her hostess. As the heiress turned to face her Lily asked, "Since all is well with you, are your surveillance days over?"

Mrs. Davenport forced a faint smile. "We'll see."

♦ ♦ ♦

"It's not based on trust, Ten. How long can a marriage like that last?"

"Sometimes forever. Some people thrive on uncertainty and unhappiness. The inspector must think Mrs. D knows more than she's told them, and you know that they're going to question you about what she told you."

"Everybody seems to be trailing everybody these days. How do I look?"

"A little more definition to the lips and you're ready for Ted and Paul Whiteman."

"Come with us, Ten. Ted will have photographs."

"You can show them to me tomorrow. Donald will come by at ten o'clock."

"Don't you feel any urgency about this case?"

"Yes, but nothing that can't wait twenty-four hours."

They reached the sidewalk just as Ted's Pontiac pulled to the curb. Ted bounded out of the vehicle.

"Hello," he said, all smiles. "You must be Tenisha. I'm glad you're coming with us. I have some questions to ask you."

The Roseland Ballroom was vast and its various levels seemed to stretch into infinity. After the waiter left with their orders, Ted pushed the glassware aside, spread photos in the center of the table and explained what they were seeing.

"This is Mr. Davenport of garage fame. No Don Juan, for sure. Here are some yearbook pictures of Jonathan Bennett. They looked like happy days for him. And here is a sketch of his father --- I couldn't ask to take his photo; what reason could I give for that? He had some beautifully mounted pictures of baseball players on the walls of his garage office. He said they were members of The Negro League. Bennett didn't strike me as an egalitarian type. He was especially keen on Rube and Willie Foster. Here are pictures I found of them."

"Did he ever go to League games?"

"Oh, yes. His eyes shone when he told me stories about their phenomenal plays."

"Did he say where he saw them play?"

"No, why, is that important?"

"Because, dear Ted, it's costly schlepping around the country, even on a chief auto mechanic's salary. Where would he get the money? And if the teams played in or near New York City, he may have dropped in on his wealthy son and on Lizette too, for that matter. I think it's worthwhile to explore the leisure activities of a man who's reputed to be dead. Your dad's a League fan, isn't he, Ten?"

"Yes, and Andrew 'Rube' Foster and his brother Willie are two of his favorite players. Dad doesn't leave for his run to Chicago until next week --- Pullman porter, Ted."

"Would he meet with us?"

"I'll ask." She rummaged through her handbag, but the young man produced a nickel first. Tenisha returned smiling. "Five o'clock dinner at Small's Paradise tomorrow night. Is that all right?" At their nod she zipped back to the telephone. When she rejoined them, she removed her jacket from the chair and waved goodbye.

"Bread and water are not dinner!" exclaimed Lily.

"I've got some work to do before I doll up for Donald, and my meatloaf will be perfect with your salad. You two are on a dinner date, your kind invitation to me, Ted, notwithstanding."

CHAPTER EIGHTEEN

"This is one of my favorite clubs. I hope you don't mind our meeting with a congenial musical background. It helps me think more clearly, and if we're talking murder clarity of thought is important. I'm Augustus Jones, Augie to my friends, and if you're Tenisha's then you're mine. Ted, Lily." He shook their hands. "Let's order a little something and then get to it." Augie Jones was delighted that Ted ordered a beer with his hamburger. "You're my man," Augie beamed. "Glad the high life you were born to hasn't spoiled you." For himself he ordered steak, mashed potatoes and carrots. He looked at the photographs on the table. "In frames, were they, that's nice. Fits well with what Rube is expecting some day, that Negroes and Whites will play side by side. Color won't matter a bit. And let me tell you, if some of our men could do it now, they'd outrun, outthrow and outpitch the best White players. Ever see James Bell play, Ted? Faster than a bullet. Amazing the way that man can run, just amazing. I wouldn't miss a game "Cool Papa" was in if I were within fifty miles of the playing field." Their beers arrived. "But getting back to Rube, that's Andrew Foster, I'm surprised that a man like Bennett would want his picture on a wall. From what Tenisha's told me, it seems that the only thing they have in common is that they're both great at what they do, Bennett as a master auto mechanic and Foster as a master pitcher for the Cuban X-Giants twenty-five-years ago. But wait, now, there was more. While Bennett was top man in someone else's company, Rube started his own. In 1910 he founded the Chicago American Giants. No club could touch them for speed, pitching or strategies. And in 1920 he founded the Negro National League, with him as president. He had eight teams, with high standards for them all. No more poor conditions or poor pay. The players could respect themselves and their part in the greatest sport there is. People came in droves to the regular games as well as the pennant races and all-star games Rube introduced. Meanwhile he was still managing the American Giants. Can you imagine —one man doing all that? He had a nervous breakdown last year, and no wonder! If Bennett admired him, he sure didn't imitate him. As for Rube's brother Willie, they got on great. Rube didn't push him into baseball, but when Willie showed talent and wanted in, Rube said okay and let him pitch for the American Giants. Fantastic pitcher. Not the kind of relationship Bennett and his son have. I could understand Bennett having White players on his walls, but Negroes? It's a puzzle."

"Were there any special characteristics about these men that might relate to Bennett?"

"Well, Lily, as I said, Rube paved the way for respect for Negroes in the game and Willie followed, but was extraordinary. Batters couldn't anticipate what pitches he would throw them because regardless of the pitch he always used the same throwing motion."

"An element of surprise. Anything else?"

"Willie pitched with his left arm."

"Bennett's a leftie," exclaimed Ted.

"But Rube pitched with his right arm. Do you know where he got those photographs, Ted, or when?"

"He said he got them as a gift two years ago, sir."

"Maybe a peace offering to a baseball lover with a message about being proud of family success, and the hard work that goes into achieving it, maybe an attempt at bonding between father and son."

"It's possible, Dad. Two years ago, Jonathan Bennett married a travel heiress, became president of her company and started La Belle Femme in Paris. He followed his dream against the odds, like the Fosters, and is in the process of succeeding."

"And he doesn't want that process disturbed. Augie, you may be right. It's possible that the hatred of father for son has become a ruse to hide an on-going relationship. Maybe some of junior's income is funding the father's leisure activities."

"Not Rube Foster for sure, Ted. As president of the Negro National League, he didn't take a penny."

"Bennett said he saw them play. Were they anywhere near New York this fall?"

Augustus pulled a neatly printed paper from his pocket. "Not near enough, Lily."

"If Bennett is cashing in on his son's wealth, you say it wasn't visible in Iowa, but if the son's life is a lie, the father's might be too. Just because his boss said he goes to Las Vegas doesn't mean he does. Did you check that out, Ted?"

"No, Tenisha, it didn't seem unreasonable."

"He was presumably in Las Vegas, for two weeks you say, covering the time that Lizette was murdered."

"Great alibi, if true Ten, but he could have hired someone to taint the cream they set aside for her. Remember, they had advance notice that she was coming in for it."

"She changed her mind, Dad, and telephoned for delivery at Singer's. That's why the police have been hounding our models, but they've also been so thorough in interrogating everyone at auntie's retail establishment that some of them threatened to quit. The ladies are in the clear. The cream must have been tainted after Lizette received it, or someone substituted a doctored look-alike jar for the real thing. She wouldn't have known the difference. This was a first-time purchase. I wish we knew what she did with it from the time she got it to the time she applied it. Who knows where she put it down or who was nearby."?

"It had to be at home, honey. It's not like powder. You don't take face cream outside the house or apply it in public."

"Well, Dad, maybe someone climbed through a window and replaced the original."

"Could be, if she lived on a low floor of her building with a fire escape and she kept her windows open or the window lock was jimmied."

"She lived on the first floor of a brownstone, Mr. Jones. I have the address. If we drive by, maybe get inside..."

"Lee, I thought we were leaving this to the police."

"Honey, then what are we doing here talking about murder and trying to figure out how Negro ballplayers can help solve the case?"

"I'll ask Uncle Harry about the windows and their proximity to the bathroom and bedroom. He's getting reluctant to talk about the case, but as his favorite niece I should be able to wheedle the information out of him. But those Negro ballplayers, hmm. If the Davenport marriage was in jeopardy, then the funding for La Belle Femme was in jeopardy, and Douglas Bennett's lifestyle, if he was cashing in, was also in jeopardy. Did he say what Las Vegas hotel he stayed in, Ted?"

"No, Lily, but I can check them all. I'll say a business deal's in jeopardy unless I can find someone who was there two days ago. I doubt if they'll give me his address, but at least I'll know if he was there. And if he was lying about this, well..."

"Thanks, Ted, and thank you Mr. Jones, Augie. Most fathers wouldn't understand a daughter getting involved in a murder case, but the victim was a fellow employee."

"Whom nobody but you liked, and this should be a police matter. What we find out we tell them." Tenisha was adamant.

Augustus Jones laughed heartily. "I do understand my daughter getting involved and denying she's involved, and doggedly sticking to the involvement and the denial, but I can't order her to stop, because what she'd stop is telling me anything about what she's doing. So, if I'm understanding at least, I'm kept informed." He looked at his watch. "I'd like to get home before your mother does, Tenisha." They rose to leave with him, but he protested, looking wistfully at Jimmy Johnson at the piano before departing.

"I wish my father were so understanding - of anything I do. I'm a lawyer's daughter, so what can he expect? He's following the case from Rochester. I telephone, reverse the charges, and he's kept more or less up to date. He worries even though Uncle Harry's here."

"Your uncle can't be much comfort. Even I know you tend to get more information than you give in any situation. At least the police haven't stopped following you."

"They may not be close enough to act fast if the murderer strikes again."

Lily grimaced. "That's reassuring, Ten. I think it's time to map the relationship of the suspects to the mystery man who seems to be the pivotal figure in poor Lizette's demise."

Ted hailed the waiter and got a large sheet of paper. "Ruth Elder step aside," said Lily, as she drew a map linking George Davenport to those whose lives he had touched. Adjectives and nouns filled the air, and Lily placed them appropriately on the paper.

"So, what conclusions do you draw from all this, Lee?"

"We have a bunch of dissatisfied people here. Charles Dupre gives George Davenport a French front, but what they have may not last. They've hooked up with the solid Singer and Martin firms, but their financing is in jeopardy if Davenport's marriage falls apart. Their control of La Belle Femme is only two years old, the length of Davenport's marriage, and not on solid enough footing, though its prospects are great, thanks in significant measure to Singer and Martin's artistry and Ruth Elder's P.R. work. Lizette was the hinge connecting Singer and Martin to La Belle Femme, and Wainwright/Davenport is the hinge keeping

La Belle Femme upright. And La Belle Femme is, artistically speaking, George Davenport. I think that the only possibility that his wife would drop her charming, lying, multinamed, poverty-born mate is if he burst her dream that he was the ideal, adoring husband. But while she's a dreamer, she's also a realist who knows she's dreaming, and killing Lizette would keep the dream going."

Tenisha jumped in. "Until another Lizette comes along. Remember, she doesn't know that he's really poor without her money and therefore not likely to stay without it. But maybe she's made a thorough investigation of his background and wants him anyway, just not with competition from another woman."

Lily came back. "Or George Davenport could have had Lizette killed so that his dream could continue. It's possible that Dupre could have done it for the same reason; this business venture means a lot to him, although his grief over Lizette's death seems genuine."

"Of course, we're dealing with a bunch of liars."

"True, Ted. I don't know if Sally found Lizette's letter to me or placed it there to implicate me, though I think her boyfriend, the lawyer, is more important to her than a financial payoff. My work at both firms that La Belle Femme is connecting with might have worried her murderer that Lizette had shared information with me that was meant to be confined to the principals of the French fashion house."

"Never mind the fashion house, Lee. Sheila Davenport could have wanted you both dead because of your possible knowledge of Lizette's relationship with her husband. If such information got out, she'd look the fool at the very least."

"I want to know the source of the letter Ben Foster had slipped under his door. Meanwhile, Ted, check whether Douglas Bennett was in Las Vegas in the past month, where he stayed and when he left."

"Will do."

"Dreams and murder." Lily shook her head. "Strange bedfellows."

"But bedfellows nonetheless, Lee, when it's 'my dream at any cost.' Shall we end with comfort food? A peach cobbler would suit me fine." Tenisha motioned to the waiter as the pianist played " Sweet Georgia Brown."

♦ ♦ ♦

Mr. Foster sat back in his chair. "You know I can't resist homemade cookies, my dear, or tea. Everyone's in such a coffee rush these days." He smiled as he poured his favorite beverage from a pot of leaves. "You're up to something, of course, something your parents would not approve of. Now what is it?" He put the cup to his lips as his eyes held Lily's.

"Dear Mr. Foster, I'm just not sophisticated or clever enough to get the information I need without arousing your suspicion."

"I wouldn't like you if you were sophisticated or clever. You're perfect just as you are, sweet, simple and constantly in trouble. No, I take that back, not simple, just uncomplicated. So, refreshing."

"Do you really see me as always in trouble?"

"A slight exaggeration to make my assistance more meaningful to me. Well, then?"

"I'd like more information about the letters, the one you received by mistake and the one Lizette wrote to me. Uncle Harry took a pledge of silence, but I'm naturally curious about whether the letters are helping the police find Lizette's murderer, and more than curious about whether they indicate my life is in danger."

"I examined all the typewriters at Wainwright Travel and was able to inform the police that the letter of warning was typed on one of their machines and with their paper, even though the ribbon imprinted with the words was long gone. The police could find no one who worked at Wainwright Travel with cause to write such a letter, with the exception of George and Sheila Davenport. They have further concluded that Mr. Davenport's checks from his account as Solomon Smith, which were used to purchase fabrics for Miss Frere, indicated an intimate relationship with her. They feel that despite his personal wealth, his wife's financial charms made a permanent or even long-term relationship with the model untenable. He may have discovered, as the police did, that his wife has employed a detective agency to track his daily whereabouts since their marriage. Apparently, she was not confident that her social reputation and her wealth could hold him. The police believe that Sheila Davenport may have prompted Miss Frere's distress note to you, and that the warning letter may have been written by either Davenport, a scare tactic by someone with a soft side, unless pushed to desperation, and therefore most probably the spouse of the murderer."

"Then the police think that one of the Davenports committed the murder?"

"They do. They do not fear for your life, since they believe you have ceased butting your amateur nose into police business and will under no circumstances go anywhere near the attractive George Davenport. Anyway, the police watch you daily, in case they're wrong. Careful man, Inspector Kirk. I was very relieved to hear you've got protection."

"You're a darling, Mr. Foster."

"I'm a worried darling, Lily. You don't go through parenthood and grandparenthood and not worry. You're my unrelated grandchild."

Lily kissed him on the cheek. "If ever I can help you..."

"I'm sure that a model or an opera singer would be a big help in my electrics business. Now listen to me. If anything frightens you, knock on my door or bang on the floor with a broom. Is that clear?"

"Very. Do have more cookies and tea."

CHAPTER NINETEEN

Tenisha took the last cookie on the plate and poured herself more tea. "I wish I had a Mr. Foster living below me. We need more information."

"The detective agency isn't likely to be much help. I doubt they'll offer information to the police that their client does not want released. Anyway, they can't know about La Belle Femme or they would have told Mrs. Davenport. She couldn't understand why her husband was willing to travel anywhere except to their newbie office in Paris, so I doubt that she knows she married a poor man, that his income, thanks to her, enabled him to start his dream business and that Lizette, besides a possible extracurricular liaison with her husband, was also a business intermediary between him, her common-law husband and La Belle Femme. Here, Ten, look at these."

Lily had placed several newspapers on the table and clipped several pages in each. Each page had a picture of Ruth Elder in La Belle Femme originals. The caption above the sumptuous coats and dresses that adorned Miss Elder read: "Coming Soon From La Belle Femme," followed by luscious descriptions of the colorful clothes, depicted in black and white, with prices that a woman with a weekly income of $40 could afford. The ad was from Wanamaker.

"What about the woman who only earns $20 a week?"

"She waits until her income doubles or she buys the Simplicity Pattern, which will undoubtedly be out soon, and makes her own."

The dress was striking, with pearl buttons running down its ankle-length, two scoop pockets tilted on either side of them and a mandarin collar.

"This will look fabulous with Mrs. Rosenthal's Maiden Form Brassiere. The respectable crowd will love it --- dignified casual, stunning."

"And the collar fits right in with the oriental Valentino craze, Ten. Coulet and Dupre have done it. They now have name recognition and appreciation and a foothold in the American market. They'll have to ramp up production. Can a two-year-old firm do that so quickly?"

"With the proper funding, Lee. Davenport can't do it on his Wainwright income, can he? And even if he could, how would he explain the drain to his wife, the mortgage company, the maids, the butlers and the chauffeurs he has to support?"

"Which brings us to Mrs. Davenport, Ten. George will probably have to invest some of her inheritance to make this expansion fly. He said he would tell her about his business at the right time, but with suspicions of a mistress and murder, is this the right time?"

"These ads indicate that he is committed to delivering merchandise now, Lee. He must already have the funding he needs. He's either stolen money from the travel business, or he's got another investor, or he's borrowed heavily with the store ads and, in a sense, Ruth Elder, as collateral, an unlikely business arrangement, I admit. Reporters would surely ask Dupre about funding, but nobody seems to realize that a La Belle Femme representative is on American soil."

"Except models and other employees of Singer and Martin, and no one's rushing to the media about this with a murder case hanging over our respective heads."

"We have to know how this expansion is being funded, Lee." Tenisha looked at her watch. "I've got to get home. Donald awaits. One telephone call and we'll have our funding answer."

"Who are you calling?"

"The newspapers. I'll use the corner telephone, to keep the request anonymous. Charles Dupre is going to be busy fielding questions tomorrow. We should have our answer soon."

♦ ♦ ♦

Ted Martin was waiting for Lily the next morning. She smiled as he gallantly dashed 'round to open the Pontiac's door for her. She felt happy that he was happy, and guilty that she had hooked him into a dangerous enterprise.

"I checked all the Las Vegas hotels. Douglas Bennett wasn't in any of them the week of the murder. Then I checked hotels in New York City. He was in a small one at that time, but that's not all." Ted stopped at a red light and turned toward Lily. "He's there now."

"What!"

"I never considered that I might be followed. I was careful this morning, but it might be too late. He's a clever, man. In one day, he may have discovered that you, I and Tenisha are trying to unravel a murder in which his son may figure prominently. Maybe he was at Roseland yesterday and saw me place the baseball pictures on the table for Tenisha's dad to see. Who knows what he's seen and what conclusions he's come to? And since the police haven't been following me, they're surely not aware of him."

"We could tell them. No, I promised George Davenport and Charles Dupre I wouldn't reveal the conversation we had in the restaurant, and that means I can't reveal his fashion business and his multiple names."

"We've gotten involved in a murder case, Lily! Dual and triple murders are not impossible. I'm not about to hire a detective. My salary won't support it, and neither will yours."

"I'll talk to Ten about it."

"What's to talk about? You know she thinks this is police business, not ours."

"I'll talk to her."

Ted pulled up to the Singer building. Lily kissed him on the cheek.

"Pick me up at five, will you?"

Ted nodded. No walk to the bus stop. She was worried too.

Tenisha, with her usual restrained good cheer, was greeting the models as they entered. As Lily passed the sign-in desk, Tenisha noted the slight uplift of her eyebrows, so fifteen minutes later she came to her to hear the Douglas Bennett news.

"We can't tell the police," Tenisha said, "That's too dangerous. He can easily outwit them --- a change of appearance and name. His son did that and more getting Singer and Martin together in the French fashion deal. We could be in trouble before they're onto him. What's the name of that hotel?" She checked the telephone book and dialed. "Mr. Douglas Bennett, please. Thank you." She replaced the receiver. "He's checked out."

"But he's just arrived!"

"He's checked out of the hotel, but I'll wager he hasn't checked out of the city."

"What shall we do?"

"We could check other hotels, but I doubt we'll find a Bennett registered in any of them. One person may be able to help us discover if we're in danger and be able to do something about it --- his son."

"But what if George Davenport himself is the danger, Ten?"
"That's a chance we have to take."

Chapter Twenty

Lily stood on the sidewalk with Tenisha looking up at the building as she had done once before. First it had been the mysterious, introspective Sheila Davenport, and now it was her even more mysterious, probably desperate husband. She and Tenisha mounted the steps, entered the building and faced the desk clerk. Their approval was immediate. Good, Lily thought, the butler had responded. The surprise would be retained until the last minute. They were admitted and shown to the sitting room, but not before hearing an earful --- of shouts, exclamations and heavy objects dropped. When the butler had departed, Tenisha rose, motioned Lily to follow and carefully and quietly moved toward the massive, ornate double doors beyond which the sounds emanated. "I'm leaving!" became ultra-clear, and as one door was thrust open the women pressed themselves flat against opposite walls. Had the shouter actually exited, they would have been seen, but a voice shouting "Stop it! Wait!" pushed the door closed. Male voices continued speaking in subdued tones, but the door was not completely shut. Tenisha and Lily inched closer to it and listened.

"You can't go on like this. You'll ruin everything."

"I'll ruin everything? I'm going to set it right. You keep secrets from me, from the world. Let them out and be done with it!"

"She won't understand. She trusts me."

"Good, good. Then she'll be supportive of you, of this enterprise."

"She trusts the man she married, George Davenport with a garage fortune, who married an equal."

"Except in the looks department."

"There's nothing wrong with her looks. Even the world would see it if she smiled more. She'll see the love of her life as a fraud. I've got to get funding somewhere else. We've got tons of orders to fill. Even in my sunniest dreams I never imagined such an instantaneous addiction to our line."

"Two years of work is instantaneous? We know she knows you were sweet on Lizette."

"That was a mistake. I let flattery and charm put a curtain between me and what was really important. If I ask her for funding she'll think the worst of me, why I married her, maybe that I killed Lizette."

"That's very possible, but if you bring her into the design fold, as partner, adviser, you can erase that fear and more."

"What 'more'?"

"I followed her yesterday and this morning. She often looked around anxiously."

"The police are following her, no doubt. I think they suspect that she may have murdered Lizette."

"Or maybe she fears that she will suffer the fate of Lizette if she gets in your way. She supports your design house and she doesn't get in the way. She's a productive part of the team."

"I don't want her to think I murdered Lizette. I don't want relationship, business or marital, based on fear. I wish the police would find who did it. Once the murderer is found I can talk to Sheila about La Belle Femme."

"You don't know when that will happen, and you need the money now. What the police find out may not be beneficial to you, Charles Dupre or the firm, but once you're back in Paris as Coulet, they can run around New York as much as they like."

"What do you mean 'not beneficial'? They can't seriously believe that Charles or I ..."

"Oh, but they can. The police are not perfect. They make mistakes, at least from time to time. Of course, your wife had as good a reason as you --- but enough of this. You wanted to see me and here I am, no possibility of phone lines being tapped by your trusting wife."

"Father, there is a source of money that you have access to. No, I'm not asking you to give me back anything. You're the pride of Davenport Garages. You're hailed and feted by the best of Iowa society --- socialites, businessmen, politicians. You can persuade one of your wealthy acquaintances to invest in La Belle Femme, a loan at prevailing rates to be repaid beginning in twelve months. All the financial statistics and sample designs, department store ads, design kudos, Ruth Elder, they'd persuade an unconscious mule. Will you do it for me, for us?"

"I would like my current lifestyle to continue, but I was planning to cash in chips due me from those people for my own account in the near future. I've cashed them in with you, my dear, devoted son, and their lives have soiled patches as well. Tapping my people to meet your needs is not a good idea."

"You're a piece of work, father. So, despite all I've done for you, you won't help me."

"I didn't say that. I like the comforts you've provided me. I just won't ask my people to subsidize your dream."

"Whom will you ask?"

"It's better that you don't know."

"You can't ask Sheila. I won't allow it."

"Did I say I would do that? Leave it to me. Before the week is out you'll have your funding. Can your staff handle questions, orders, shipments, accounting in Dupre's absence?"

"Not well. He's got to get back to Paris, but the police won't let him leave. Me they can live without for a while, the designs are on the assembly line and ready to roll, but without the vice-president and accountant at headquarters instead of the elite, classy well-run firm we are we'll look like a bunch of amateurs. From the calls Charles and I have gotten in the last day or two, it looks like that perception has begun already."

"I'll get Charles Dupre back to Paris. No questions. I said I'll do it, and you know I do what I say. This is goodbye for now." He held out his hand, and his son took it and shook it firmly.

Tenisha and Lily moved quickly and quietly back to the sitting room. They stood behind its door and peeked beyond it to watch a thin, hawk-nosed man pass into the foyer. They heard the door open and "Good day, sir," before they hurried to intercept the butler on his way to the room that held George Davenport.

"Don't announce us," said Tenisha. "We'll return at a more agreeable time for Mr. Davenport," said Lily, and they almost leapt to the front door. Lily's hand was on its handle when she and Tenisha exchanged looks that spoke their intentions. "But I will at least pay my respects to Mr. Davenport before I leave," said Lily, as Tenisha made a quick exit, entering the elevator featuring Douglas Bennett just before its door closed.

"Mr. Davenport will see you in the study, Miss." Lily followed the butler, who closed the door behind her.

"Thank you for seeing me." Lily shook a hand George Davenport hadn't offered. "I seem to have appeared at a bad time." Davenport displayed a second of alarm. "You have so much work to do." She eyed the desk which, despite her distance, she knew held the brochures, reviews, testimonials, advertisements that Bennett had refused to take as funding catnip for his son's design house.

"In a way I'm glad you've come. I would like to apologize for my sharp retorts to your questions in the restaurant. I'm usually more civil."

"I accept your apology, and I know you're more civil. Miss Jones was impressed with your charm, your intelligence, and your knowledge ranging from auto mechanics to women's clothing when she first met you at A'Lelia Walker's party. And if I were suspected of murder my retorts would be equally as sharp, and I would be equally as sorry, so I'm pleased that at least in that way you're glad I've come, but may I ask in what way you are not glad I've come?"

Davenport stared at her intently for a moment. "You may, but first tell me why you have come."

"First, to thank you for warning me that the result of involvement in this murder case can be deadly. You did write me that warning note, didn't you?"

"You seem to think so, and the police seem to think so."

"Are we right?"

"It was written on Wainwright stationery and on a Wainwright typewriter, so I must have done."

"Your wife ---"

"Did not write it."

"You wrote, 'the force aligned against you cannot allow you to succeed.' You know, then, who that force is?"

"No, as I told the police, I know what that force is. Jealousy is a terrible force, terrible as in terror. It can be deadly because only the emotions are involved, and emotions don't think. Lizette Frere was a beautiful and elegant woman. She did not make female friends easily outside her mileu, across the ocean in a city that understands and appreciates real women."

"So, another woman took her life, perhaps a model at Singer Couture, or someone on staff at Walter Martin or someone in her apartment building."

"It's reasonable to assume that."

"Extremely jealous women may be pushed to murder, but apparently not your wife, whose extremes, if any, reside in a rational intellect and humanitarian work."

"Exactly."

"So, you don't believe Lizette's murder was La Belle Femme related?"

"How could it be? No one, present company excepted, was aware of her work for my design firm, and I thank you also for keeping that information private until I am ready for the world to know. Perhaps I shouldn't be telling you this, but the model Sally is suspected of some involvement in Lizette's death. Her fingerprints were on Lizette's letter to you in addition to yours."

"That explains why she looked so wild-eyed this morning. And you expect me to believe that pretty, uncomplicated Sally is the unremitting force that cannot allow me to succeed in discovering the murderer?"

"I don't care what you believe, as long as it's not that I or my wife or Dupre had anything to do with it."

"My neighbor downstairs, Mr. Foster, takes a fatherly interest in me. We know each other, and we see each other often. I don't know you at all. Why should you have a particular interest in my welfare?"

"Perhaps some of my wife's humanitarian caring has rubbed off on me."

Lily stood up. "I'm now asking why you are not glad I came."

"Because it bothers me that your suspicions still extend to me and my personal and business relationships, and I admit to displeasure that you are here in my home, first to speak to my wife without her request, and now to do likewise with me. This visit would be especially embarrassing if my wife were to return, which she shall within the hour, and find you here. Even a sensible woman in complete control of her emotions would feel uncomfortable having a beautiful, uninvited lady appear in her husband's study when he knows she will be away. An erroneous conclusion can easily be reached by even the most sanguine wife. The two of us together with the door shut ---"He looked up. "Oh, hello, darling."

Sheila Wainwright Davenport stood in the doorway. "Have you come to see me again, Miss Chasen?"

"No, Mrs. Davenport. I thought I'd give your husband equal time. My immediate concern is to allay my latent fear of becoming the next murder victim."

"Why do you think there will be a second one?"

"Because the murder of Lizete Frere has complicated rather than resolved the problem the murderer faces."

"You know who the murderer is?" exclaimed George Davenport.

"I have a strong suspicion, as does one of you."

"Which one?" asked Sheila Davenport.

"Of that I'm not sure."

"If you have nothing to say to me, Miss Chasen, I'm tired and must ask you to leave."

"Certainly. Please pardon this intrusion."

In the elevator Lily prayed for Tenisha's safety. As she exited the desk clerk was on the telephone. He hung up, wrote in a book and turned to greet a stylish couple. Lily leaned over the desk as she passed. She read, "Under no circumstances is Lily Chasen to be admitted to this building."

♦ ♦ ♦

Bennett hailed a taxicab, and Tenisha followed in another. She glanced unseeing out a side window as the taxi, one behind Bennett's, stopped for a light. The father was about to play a crucial role for his son as facilitator. Without his intervention La Belle Femme might just grind to a halt. He would provide an infusion of capital, and get a key administrator back on the job, but how?

"Stop here!" A block ahead Bennett had alighted from his taxi. She paid the driver as she watched Bennett enter Dupre's hotel. She pulled off her stylish hat and entered the lobby after him, standing boldly by his side at the desk as he asked for Dupre. The clerk looked at the key rack. It was #21C, but # 21D also held a key.

"I'm sorry, sir, Mr. Dupre is out. Would you care to leave a message?"

"No, I'll wait." Bennett took a leather seat in the corner and folded his arms.

Tenisha spoke, a Southern accent flowing from her lips. "I'm here for 21D, personal maid."

The desk clerk displayed mild surprise.

"Pays very well," said Tenisha, fingering the stylish raccoon collar she thought would impress George Davenport.

"He certainly does," responded the desk clerk.

Tenisha was not pleased. Personal maid, or more, to a man. No doubt the desk clerk thought the worst. "I'd like to prepare his evening wardrobe before he returns."

"I'm sorry, but I have no instructions to admit anyone. You'll have to wait."

"Ladies room?"

"In the back to your right."

Tenisha hurried to the rear of the lobby, made a right and entered the last in a bank of elevators. As she exited, she paused. presumably to look for something in her purse, until the elevator door closed. She scanned the room doors for an open one and followed her ears to a vacuum cleaner down one of the corridors. A maid looked up as she entered.

"Could you help me? I know I'm a bit early, but I'd like to get in and freshen up. Personal maid, 21D."

The floor maid looked her over, as had the desk clerk, and walked her down another corridor. She flipped through dozens of keys, before opening 21D. "Personal maid, huh!" she muttered, as she left.

Tenisha looked around the room. Old World class. She walked to the wall separating 21D from 21C. She moved a sofa and chair a foot away from it and ran her fingers the width and height of it as far as she could reach. She knelt to feel the baseboard until her examination reached waist height. There were several dents in the plaster that might give way with a little assistance, but the one at sofa height looked best for drilling. Apparently continual shoving into the wall had found a weak spot. She reached for the telephone.

"Personal maid, 21D, screwdriver and hammer, please. Thank you." The floor maid delivered them almost immediately. The hotel didn't have its sterling reputation for nothing. She drilled, then stopped and listened for about five minutes before she heard the door beyond slam shut. With the pillows that extended above sofa height the hole she'd made would be invisible. She moved the sofa farther from her, sat on the floor, clasping her knees, and put her ear to the 2" hole.

"Circumventing the police here, Mr. Bennett, is difficult to do. They are a tenacious lot. I tried two weeks ago and couldn't even board a plane in Boston."

"I can get you on a plane to Paris, Mr. Dupre, and it is important that I do. At the inauguration of La Belle Femme's line to the American market, we cannot allow it to fail."

"We?"

"Fear not, Mr. Dupre, I have no interest in partnering with you and my son, and no interest whatsoever in fashion. Fashion is my son's fire, mine is the financial reward that a generous son bestows on his father. Don't look so surprised. The promise of financial reward is what has made this country great. It requires creative talent and business acumen. You and my son are perfect for each other, and I am here to applaud and assist you."

"How do you intend to get me to Paris?"

"There is a train leaving for Chicago in the morning. You and I shall be on it. Tomorrow night there is a flight from

Chicago to Paris, with stops in Boston and New York City. No need to worry. If the police check for you in either city they will check those boarding, not those on board. When I leave you, I will purchase two tickets for the morning train and, when we arrive, one ticket for the flight to Paris."

"I appreciate what you're doing for us, Mr. Bennett, even if your reasoning is foreign to me. Is there no love in you for the aesthetic arts for their own sake?"

"Not that I'm aware of. Jonathan received artistic interest and talent from his mother. If she were still here, I might bend slightly toward its appreciation, but she is not. I pride myself in being an expert in science, the science of the fastidious accumulation of money and the treats it can buy. I'm a collector, Mr. Dupre, but not a boastful one. I don't say, 'See what I've done?' It is enough that I see it, that I know it, that I have the satisfaction of having carefully used my mind to bring it about."

"George told me that your wife died in an operating room."

"Yes, the medical science of saving lives failed her. The doctors, who make fortunes whether their patients live or die, took her from me. They weren't worthy of their craft, their science. When I repair an automobile, I do not release it until it is in pristine condition. I do not accept that it can be in any but pristine condition after I have worked on it. Don't be alarmed, Mr. Dupre. I mean no harm to anyone who means no harm to those I love."

"I see the truth of what you say in police science. They are unable to find the murderer of my Lizette. She was serving our company and died for it."

"The police seem to think that she was serving herself with your partner, my son, which I don't believe for a moment, but they grasp at social straws when their science fails them. They can't understand that for some people the craft of business can overwhelm all other considerations."

"You've read the newspaper stories, heard from George, can your scientific mind explain the murder of Lizette?"

"Yes, it can. She was unique, a French model at an American design firm, and the other models paled by comparison. She was on track for advancement at Singer and for even more lucrative positions elsewhere. The other models hated her, and the business manager there even more so."

"Except for Lily Chasen. Lizette appreciated her friendship."

"Yes, Miss Chasen was the only one who feigned to like her."

"Feigned? What do you mean? I've spoken to her. She's a fine person who was much attached to Lizette."

"What if she were clever enough to hide her dislike with smiles and friendship so that when a horrible death befell her 'friend' she would not be suspected of perpetrating it."

"She was suspected, at first. You've never met her. You do not understand."

"As you wish. You asked, and I'm giving you my amateur viewpoint for what it's worth, perhaps not much, as you say. May I use the telephone?"

Tenisha heard Bennett call the railroad station.

"Be at the station at 10:30 in the morning. The train leaves at 10:35. Tonight, very late, tell the desk to awaken you at noon. You will be able to get to the station unnoticed by the police, and by the desk, too, if you leave by the side exit. Even if the police suspect you've fled, they will not expect you to be boarding a train to Chicago. I'll see you at the station. Goodbye."

Tenisha stood upright, her muscles aching. Bennett was a strange man who could bring danger into innocent lives. She pushed the sofa back in place and mounted the pillows high on it. She heard a key turn and rushed behind the door. As it opened, and someone with a heavy footstep entered the room, she quickly made her exit before the man turned to shut the door.

Chapter Twenty-One

Bernard Singer stood, more rumple-haired than usual, in front of the models seated at the tables to the left of the runway.

"You shouldn't be here, and I shouldn't be here. We should be about our business, which is not getting done because of the distraction of a lovely young lady's murder. I want her murderer caught as much as anyone, but I can't allow our fashion business to suffer because justice has not yet been done Lizette. None of you have been yourselves of late. There's been too much whispering in the workrooms and too much fear coming down the runway. Clients have commented on it. I had no idea until the police investigation that none of you liked her. You were supposed to like her! You girls are supposed to get on well together. I won't allow you to get into social snits. When you do and a murder occurs, you're all suspects and the business is damaged. It's too late now to set things to rights with our unfortunate French model, but if ever there is another murder on these premises, I expect to hear that you all adored the deceased! Is that clear? When I question you, I expect total honesty? I am now about to question you. Does anyone here dislike anyone employed at Singer?"

"Oh, dear," thought Lily, as eyes darting everywhere made the competitive spirit clear. Tenisha's eyes were fixed firmly on the floor.

"This is not good," declared Singer. "Get over it! That's an order! Now get back to work. Margaret, Lee, come here. Margaret, you've been very hard on Lee since she arrived. What don't you like about her?"

"Nothing in particular. I don't dislike her any more than any of the other girls, but she does keep Tenisha from her work. She drops by to speak to her many times during the day."

"For how long?"

"Oh, maybe a minute, but it's not the length of time but the number of times she does it. When Tenisha's working on figures I don't want her concentration broken."

"Has she made errors, not finished her work on time?"

"No, but ---"

"Then drop it! The girls are allowed passing pleasantries. We have not taken vows of silence. Lee, what can Margaret do to make amends for her social disregard?"

Lily thought for a moment, then looked an apoplectic Margaret in the face. "As a former bookkeeper I am curious about the checks Singer and La Belle Femme exchanged in the course of their business relationship. I'd like to see them."

"Are you crazy? What business is it of yours?" Margaret was about to burst.

"Just curious. Figures used to be my business. Allowing me to see them would indicate that you trust me, that you truly welcome me as a model at Singer."

"Odd," said Bernard Singer, "but I get your drift, and I see no harm in it. What do you say, Margaret?"

Margaret Singer was too stunned to respond.

"Good! That's settled. I expect to see you smiling at each other from now on. Margaret, show her the books immediately, so that we can get back to work."

Margaret marched silently to her office, Lily following, past a bewildered Tenisha outside Margaret Singer's sanctuary waiting to speak to her boss. When Lily left twenty minutes later, she slipped Tenisha a paper just as her friend slipped her one. They both said, "lunch."

♦ ♦ ♦

"I've got lots to tell you, but I'm dying to hear about your conversation with George Davenport and what in the world you were doing in Margaret's office."

"It was Margaret's peace offering, which her brother allowed and she daren't refuse, that I could examine payments between La Belle and Singer. La Belle's checks went to Singer, and at first Singer's checks went to Paris, but about five months ago ten percent of Singer's reimbursement for La Belle expenses went to someone billed as La Belle's U.S. agent in Iowa City, Iowa. From what Ted said and what you and I heard from behind closed doors, Douglas Bennett does not seem to be a man who takes gratuities on faith."

"You're so right! I followed him to Dupre's hotel and listened from next door. Dad's off on a Chicago run tomorrow and Dupre and Bennett will be on the train. Dupre is leaving for Paris from Chicago! I've got to tell Dad to keep an eye on them. Menu, menu! What can we eat that won't interfere with our conversation?"

♦ ♦ ♦

"You didn't have to do it yourself, Mr. Foster. I would gladly have paid one of your men to do it."

"I trust my employees, of course, but I had to make sure that there actually was a telephone to install and that the installation actually took place. Your charm, my dear, can dissuade men from doing what they are supposed to do, more-so when you tip generously for their obedience. I recall the refrigerator you thought took up too much room, and which I had to persuade you could function in multiple ways."

Lily blushed and looked at that item, its top lined with books, its metal doors festooned with assorted messages held in place by colorful magnets and its handles embraced by silk stockings, the lines frozen straight.

"My mistake was continually asking if I could gift you with a telephone. Your parents were wiser. They just sent you one."

"They're darlings, but they should be saving for their retirement."

"They're worried, and rightly so, and a father who's an attorney can well afford to save for that far-off day and buy his daughter a telephone, and I'm sure you can afford the fifty cents a month to maintain it. Now call your parents, tell them you love them and that the telephone looks classy and gorgeous. The whole city's gone wild for French telephones, and since it's the fashion you should have been in the forefront of buyers, not bringing up the rear. I won't mention the obvious fact that for someone who's stuck her nose more than necessary in a murder puzzle a telephone is an essential means of protection."

"Yes, Mr. Foster."

"Is that 'yes' agreement to calling your parents immediately and to recognizing the truth of what I've just said, or to getting me to leave with the impression that you agree with me, whether you do or not."

"Yes, yes, and yes. Dear Mr. Foster, you will always be deep in my affections, and you will always be a 'yes' to me."

Ben Foster shook his head, sighed and shuffled to the door. He turned. "Come here." Lily did, and he kissed her on the head and left.

Lily's father was delighted that she had acted quickly in installing the telephone, and her mother told her that progress on her winter gloves was proceeding well. Mrs. Chasen was aware that her daughter could afford to purchase a stylish pair, but this would be a reminder of family, of Rochester, of home.

The gold and white telephone looked smashing. Lily felt slightly embarrassed to be wearing a comfy, old robe in its presence. She poured herself a cup of tea from the glazed pink floral teapot, another gift from her mother, and pushed the wingback chair closer to the little table and the small fireplace which had first attracted her to the apartment. She had wanted that and a little garden, and had gotten both, one in her apartment and the other outside Mr. Foster's apartment below hers. She could look at the lovely table, chairs and flowers below her window and holding them warmly in her heart sit in her own chair in front of her own fireplace to dream, think and read. On her table lay HAMLET. It seemed appropriate. A family murder. George Davenport had a father in his old family, and a wife and her social set as well as his dream business in his new family. Someone in one of his families, or tangential to it had murdered a business and personal friend. Lily sipped the tea. Who had the best motive for murder? It could have been someone at Singer or Martin, but their motives paled beside those of family. Of course, what may seem outwardly pale could be magnified in the mind of a deranged person. Divorce, competition and bribery were more normal ways of coping with perceived infidelity. Dupre, Wainwright and Bennett could have used them all to advantage, and she and Tenisha knew that Bennett had certainly used one of them. Dupre and Wainwright would have been embarrassed if Lizette had taken up with their partners, but murder is not a normal outcome of embarrassment. Mrs. Davenport's feeling of insecurity did border on the paranoid; she must have spent a small fortune since the onset of her two-year marriage having her husband's whereabouts and activities tracked.

She seemed more the dreamer and Dupre more the realist. Lily did not think him likely to jeopardize his business success for a woman, and if the French reputation was correct, Lizette would not have fallen to pieces if Dupre had done to her what it was perceived she had done to him. And Bennett seemed a wily realist, getting even with his son by cashing in on his success. But a Lizette & George affair might have derailed the revenge and the cash flow if Mrs. Davenport had tightened the purse strings or expelled George. And George Davenport, would he have ended a sidebar affair with murder? He hardly seemed the type, but his dream was on the verge of crashing unless Lizette backed off, unless Charles got her to back off for the good of them all. But what if the face cream delivered to her at Singer Couture was meant for someone else? Several of the models were using it, including Sally. Could Lizette herself have doctored it to rid herself of someone who disliked her intensely which was most of the models? But her note to Lily... Could she have feared that someone at Singer wanted her dead? Did George and Sheila Davenport have nothing at all to do with her demise? Perhaps this would be one of those cases that go on forever unsolved, until by chance one day someone would remember something, find something when those involved were long gone from this mortal life. The tea was getting cold, and Lily rose for more, warming on the stove. She sat down to lamplight at her elbow, a comforting crackle from the fireplace and HAMLET. Maybe this is not the best reading for an evening, she thought. She closed the book and turned on the radio. Paul Whiteman and his orchestra would soon be on with cheery music. She would imagine she was there in person, dancing with Ted as per the night before. It wasn't that she didn't like other people and other music at this hour, it was that when she had developed a happy habit, she preferred to retain it, and happy habits were a wonderful counterpoint to murder. Just as Whiteman's show was announced, the telephone rang.

"What are you doing now?" It was Tenisha.

"I was going to listen to Paul Whiteman."

"Well, listen to me first. Dad just called from Chicago. Dupre and Bennett got off there. I guess Bennett will wait for a connecting train to Iowa City. It's due in an hour. I got an earful from Dad about their behavior on the train. Meet me at Jelly's on Fourteenth Street. They're open late tonight, and you love their key lime pie."

"I'd rather not have dessert calories take up residence in me for the night."

"Weight never shows on you."

"I hope you crossed your fingers when you said that. I don't want you jinxing my metabolism. You're usually not in such a rush."

"Tomorrow's a busy day. Four clients are coming in for personal showings morning and afternoon, and Margaret wants to go over this month's expenditures with me."

"I just did that with her this morning. Well, she was standing there while I did it for myself."

"That's why it's odd, and it's not the end of the month. But we won't be able to talk until we leave work."

"All right, but I'm making it a low-calorie night. Goodbye, Paul Whiteman!"

"You heard him yesterday in person. What's the big deal?"

Lily sighed. Didn't anyone understand? "See you in thirty minutes."

Ten minutes later, keys in hand, Lily was about to exit her apartment when the telephone rang. She was beginning to think that a telephone was a better acquisition in theory than in reality. Forget "hello."

"Yes?"

"Dad called again. The train has started back to New York. As he walked down the aisle to the dining car, he stepped aside to let someone pass. It was Douglas Bennett."

CHAPTER TWENTY-TWO

The night was extremely dark. If the North Star was in the sky, it was in hiding. Lily walked to the bus stop, grateful that many couples were strolling that Thursday night and that Tony's Luncheonette was well-lit and busy. Only a five-minute wait, and the bus was on time. As she took a seat, various scenarios of what Tenisha's father had to say played through her head. The half block to Jelly's was happily filled with people, and she entered the dessert emporium with relief. She looked around the popular cafe. Perhaps her friend had been held back by telephone calls too. The waiter escorted her to a table. She ordered a green tea and waited. Five minutes. Ten minutes. This was so unlike Tenisha. She asked to use the telephone. She hung up the receiver and dialed Ted.

"Ted, I can't reach Ten. She was supposed to meet me at Jelly's ten minutes ago. I telephoned and she's not picking up. Go to her apartment. If she's there, call me. If she's not there, call the police."

◆ ◆ ◆

Jelly's could not have looked more beautiful to Lily than it did thirty minutes later when Ted entered with Tenisha. Lily ran to hug her. "What happened?" she breathed.

Tenisha sighed heavily, plopped into a seat, ordered a whiskey and soda, and didn't speak until it had arrived and she had taken a deep drink. She shook her head and put her right hand to her heart.

"Thank God for Ted! I was afraid to leave the building! I looked out the window and saw someone leaning against the lamppost across the street. Five minutes later he was still there. I couldn't call you; I knew you had already left. If I wasn't at the bus stop in five minutes, I'd have to wait half an hour for the next bus. It was only half a block, so I decided to be brave. I walked down to the lobby, opened the front door, and as I did so, the figure at the lamppost started walking toward me. I dashed back up the stairs, locked myself in, ran to the telephone and waited. At the slightest movement at my door, I was calling the police. After five minutes I went to the window. There he was, leaning against the lamppost. I knew you'd be worried, but what could I do? What a relief when I recognized Ted's gorgeous Pontiac parking in front of my building."

"It's not the best model," apologized Ted.

"Gorgeous, gorgeous!" exclaimed Tenisha.

"I looked up, saw the light in Ten's window and movement behind the curtain. Just one figure moving, and it looked like hers. The street was empty, except for me and a man smoking a cigarette and standing under the lamppost. I reached for the crowbar I keep under the seat and shoved it into a pocket." Their eyes were on those deep raccoon coat pockets. "Then I got out of the car and walked toward the man. 'Are you waiting for someone?' I asked. 'What business is it of yours, he said. 'I don't like strangers hanging around my girlfriend's building at night for no reason, so move on.' He glared at me. 'I've as good a right to stand here as you have, so go about your business and leave me to mine. I'm entitled to lounge until my wife's friend leaves, a male friend you understand. If I enter now there will be unpleasantness, and I prefer to remain a peaceful man.' I reached into my coat pocket and slowly moved the crowbar almost to the surface. When he saw that, he backed off with his hands palms up toward me and walked down the street. I walked after him, which made him walk faster, but before he drove off, I noted his license plate number. I hurried to my car to write it down. Then I ran up three flights and called Tenisha loudly through the door. And that's it, and we're only thirty minutes late."

Key lime pie never tasted so good to Lily as the trio settled in to hear Tenisha's tale, told her by her father, a tale of Charles Dupre and Douglas Bennett on a train to Chicago.

"They were a very odd pair," began Tenisha. "Dad said they didn't seem to know each other. Dupre would order a gin and tonic and Bennett would say 'You like that stuff?' Bennett sneered at Dupre's beef bourguignon, julienned carrots and truffles and ordered roast beef and mashed potatoes. He nearly choked laughing at the flaming crepes Suzette. He had ordered apple pie and ice cream. Dupre didn't respond, but looked increasingly agitated. Dad felt sorry for him and offered him the braised beets he was delivering to another table. He said it was on the house."

"Your father's a porter; why was he delivering food?"

"He switched with one of the waiters, so that the youngster could feel what it was like to be a porter and he could keep an eye on Bennett and Dupre, but his boss passed by and was furious. Fortunately, Dad has seniority and does marvelous apologies. Dupre did not appreciate that Bennett's idea of comfort meant sprawling into his space in the observation car. Dad passed by as often as he could, but neither said much. Bennett did pull out a writing pad and write something on it. Dad said it looked like figures, and after he had passed him and looked back, he saw Dupre take out his wallet and pull some bills from it."

"Sounds like Dupre got some rough verbal and financial treatment from his fellow traveler."

"I'll bet he telephones a complaint to Davenport."

"Maybe not, Ten. Bennett found a way to get him out of the country, and Davenport isn't fond of his father either. Why give him more cause for dismay? And remember, Bennett told his son he would get him the money La Belle Femme needs to see it through this awkward time. He'll need at least a year's worth of funding before the firm is on solid financial footing. Then, if he signs some long-term contracts the company can manage on its own."

"Yes, Lee, and perhaps not need the Wainwright fortune to sustain it. Even if Davenport isn't borrowing from the company coffers, he may feel like a parasite relying on Wainwright security."

"So Mrs. Wainwright is the third wheel."

"It's not a bad idea to have a spare. Auto Mechanics 101. But Bennett said he wouldn't ask her, Lee."

"No, he didn't. When George told him not to, he said, 'Would I do that?' He might! If he's not going to ask his Iowa cronies for the money, where else can he get it?"

"He's coming back with Dad on the Chicago to New York run. If we could follow him when he gets off the train we could find out."

"Well, we can't. You and I are working girls."

"And I'm a working guy," piped up Ted.

"If Sheila Davenport were a friendlier sort, we might persuade her to set detectives on Bennett's tail. She seems to be making a hobby of it. She's probably set detectives on each of us."

"Possibly. We're both too nosey, and you're a model. Lizette was a threat, and maybe you are too."

"And you, you could be another Josephine Baker, a star attraction to one and all, including her husband."

"Why not? If the American Baker can become a hot French property, why can't this American Negro become a hot French model? Oh, but the French attraction would be a more compelling argument for her if she knew that her husband is Coulet, of soon-to-be French fashion fame. She's pivotal in this murder case, and I think Bennett knows it."

"Ted, would you be a dear and find out which hotel Bennett is staying in?"

"When, Lily, during my lunch hour?"

"Oh, would you? You're a darling! And would you trace the identity of the detective and his agency from the man's driver's license?"

Ted scowled, and Lily amended the request.

"Just the hotel, then. Give me the license number and I'll check it out, and then we can inform Inspector Kirk. The police ought to know."

"Why does 'and then' come after we do the work?" growled Ted.

"Give up," Tenisha whispered to him, as Ted pulled out some bills and motioned to the waiter.

Chapter Twenty-Three

"You know, Miss Chasen, you've gotten to be a liability in this murder case. WE ask the suspects questions, not you. Murder investigations are our profession. We don't model, and we don't expect you to investigate. You don't die from showing too much leg on the runway, but butt in to something for which you have no background and you just might. Sergeant Chasen did his duty in informing us of your inquiries, and we have investigated. In the future, bypass your uncle and ask me directly if you have any concerns about the welfare of yourself or your friend." He nodded toward Tenisha. "I expect the future for this case to be relatively short. We've investigated Mrs. Davenport's activities and found them to be both extensive and reprehensible. She considered all models at this firm to be a threat to her marriage, and so had all of them followed, at enormous expense. It would have been more profitable for her had she bought the A-1 Detective Agency. She eventually reduced the number of detectives under hire to two, one for you, Miss Chasen, and one for you, Miss Jones. You're both entitled to sue her for invasion of privacy, unless, of course, you do or did have a personal involvement with her husband. I'm sorry to say that our men, who followed you in their professional capacities, took a while to realize that you, Miss Chasen, were being followed, and never realized, Miss Jones, that you were followed as well, until Ted Martin informed us of that fact. In future, for your protection, you will be followed by men on the police force. Here are the daytime lookouts for you, Miss Chasen, and for you, Miss Jones." He put photos on the table. "I want you to know to whom to look for help until we arrest the murderer of Lizette Frere. It won't be long now."

"How did you come to whatever conclusion you've come to?"

"I don't care to share that at this time, Miss Jones, but we have almost all the information we need. Just a few more 'nails in the coffin,' so to speak, and we're done. You have the same information, which you acquired in your admirable though amateurish way. Jonathan Bennett was poor, alienated his father, married well, and needs to stay married to continue to live well. We know that his wife is inordinately concerned about her marriage, her social standing, and her self-esteem, and that she dreads being the butt of gossip or jokes which she endured as a child. Surely you have an inkling of where these facts lead."

"Did you interview the father?"

"Of course, Miss Chasen. He was distraught that his son's gifts as an auto mechanic had gone to waste, but he has come to peace with a young man who is an adventurer at heart with a spirit of wanderlust, a male flapper, if you will, who has settled in to a marriage that can support his flapper instincts. Mrs. Davenport, through her own investigations, which mirrored ours, has discovered the truth about his real identity, and the father says he rests easy knowing that he was not to blame for the revelation. Surely, young ladies, you see where this investigation is leading and the limited possibilities for murderer that it presents."

"So you see Mr. Davenport's goal as the one he enjoys now, the good life and Wainwright Travel?" asked Tenisha.

"What else? Ah, to have achieved one's dream so young, but at what cost? And his wife ... The case will conclude soon. Just a few more nails, as I said."

"Are you implying that the pair of them were involved in Lizette's demise, that George Davenport enjoyed her and he and his wife destroyed her for the sake of their marriage?""

"Why so shocked, Miss Jones? But then models don't live in the real world."

"I'm not a model, I'm a bookkeeper and financial assistant, and I see the world very clearly, thank you. Your conclusions may be premature. Those extra nails may not appear, or be too bent to secure the coffin."

"You seem to like the Davenports, Miss Jones."

"I've met them and I like them."

"Merely met them? And perhaps you have a preference for one?"

Lily looked down, grit her teeth and closed her eyes.

"Perhaps," replied Tenisha.

"May I venture to guess that it is Mr. Davenport?"

"You may venture to guess whatever you like, Inspector."

"Missing coffin nails, Miss Jones? I think not."

"May we get back to work, Inspector?"

"That you may." He rose from the chair and stretched.

"Since this is the company lounge, and young, attractive women will soon be pouring in for the morning break, you may want to hasten your exit. It might be deemed inappropriate in your professional capacity to be seen in such a social, unreal world setting, especially so early in the morning."

"I'm leaving, Miss Jones, but before I do, it is very appropriate that I check to see if any alcohol is part of the girls' morning break."

"They're women," corrected Tenisha, "and the Supreme Court of the State of New York has ruled that the police are not empowered to enforce the abstinence legislation."

Inspector Kirk forced a smile. "As you say." And he was gone.

"Oh, Tenisha!" wailed Lily.

"I couldn't help it. He can't prove my involvement with the Davenports, except for butting into his business, and he's certainly not doing his business all that well. He doesn't know about La Belle Femme. Bennett held that back. He doesn't know and Mrs. Davenport doesn't know."

"Well, at least he's doing something right, protecting us, though after the tongue-lashing you gave him, he may skimp on protecting you." She looked at her watch. "Meeting time. I'm dying to know what Margaret found in the books that she wants to talk to you about."

"Please don't use that word 'dying.'" And they separated at the door, Lily for a modeling session for a newlywed and Tenisha for Margaret's office.

◆ ◆ ◆

A gentle breeze was blowing and the tulips were swaying to and fro in the tiny park one block from Singer Couture. Lily and Tenisha had unwrapped their sandwiches and uncapped their soda bottles.

"The big deal is that the monthly check going to 'Agent, Iowa City' became a weekly check last month, just for that month. It's back to normal now. I told Margaret that I wasn't doing some costly, creative accounting. The boss said do it, so I did it. La Belle Femme authorized extra checks to Bennett for no reason at all. Bernie didn't care why. It was a temporary extra cost of doing business with Coulet's firm. We know that Bennett was in New York City, not in Las Vegas, during the week Lizette was murdered last month. Lizette's cream was hand-delivered, and she's not here to describe who delivered it. If three of Bennett's checks were necessary to hire a chemist to doctor the cream, reseal it and deliver it or get someone else to deliver it, he'd get additional checks. He's not the kind of man who would use his own extorted income."

"But if the check came from La Belle Femme, then Davenport and Dupre knew what it was going for."

"Maybe Bennett didn't specify, and they were in no position to get answers Bennett refused to provide. They were, after all, being blackmailed."

"Ten, Davenport may be involved in the murder. I didn't think he was, but if he gave his father carte blanche and he used it to murder Lizette, then Davenport played a part in her death."

"Don't rush the end of the story, Lee. Let's wait to see who Bennett sees and what he does when he returns to the city."

"You're right, my ever-practical friend. Is 'friend' okay to use now?"

Tenisha flashed one of her rare, warm smiles. "It's okay. If you didn't think Davenport was a party to murder, who did you think was?"

"Bennett."

"Me too. Nasty man. I think he was at least an accessory, but we'll have a better idea of the truth once his train arrives," she glanced at her watch, "in eight hours and fifteen minutes. We can't disregard Sheila Davenport, although she has my sympathy. She may have used cosmetics for revenge on the object of her husband's wandering eyes. If we're diligent and patient we'll see the truth emerge. You made your tuna sandwich, right? You didn't buy it?" Lily nodded. "Good. For a while we'd better eat food we've prepared. Beware not only cosmetics, but butter, mayo, mustard, ketchup and all other connectives and spices."

They threw their paper bags and bottles into the trash bin.

"Time to get back to my pedestal," said Lily.

"And me merely to my desk. Lucky you."

CHAPTER TWENTY-FOUR

It was five o'clock, and a dozen chattering young women were exiting Singer Couture. Sally tapped Lily on the shoulder and pulled her aside. Tenisha walked on.

"The police seem to talk to you a lot, well more than to the rest of us. Do they think I had more to do with Lizette's letter than I've said?"

"The police are on to juicer evidence. You don't have to worry, Sally,"

"Thanks, Lee. If I were arrested, it would look bad for my boyfriend, an attorney with a girlfriend suspected of murder, you know."

"I know. Don't worry, you're not a serious suspect. Go see a movie, something happy and romantic. Get your man to turn his thoughts to marriage, instead of his career and those murder movies Mr. Future District Attorney likes to see."

"Thanks, Lee, thanks so much," and she hurried away.

Sally as the wife of an attorney? Well, thought Lily, he wouldn't have to worry about her getting into his business, but he better have a strong table for her to jump onto if she sees a mouse. When he gets home she'll have a big, strong attorney to protect her and the kids. And what about her macho man? He had done well for Ten the other day. He had possibilities, but so did she, and she had to make sure he didn't forget that. She rejoined Tenisha waiting patiently at the door.

♦ ♦ ♦

"Ted, where have you been?" Lily spoke anxiously into the receiver.

"I stayed in my office working the telephone book and the telephone. If Douglas Bennett came in on the 6:15 from Chicago he must be sleeping on a park bench. I've called every major hotel in the city, and some not so major, and he hasn't checked in. A man doesn't wander the city for five hours with luggage."

"He only had an overnight case."

"Maybe he checked it at a girly bar and is having a night of raucous entertainment. I'd check the brothels, if I knew where they were. My education is somewhat limited."

"I can understand his sticking with Dupre to make sure nothing occurred to prevent him from boarding the plane to Paris. What I want to know is why he came back. He's been somewhere for five hours, but where?"

"I have no idea, but I'm going home to get some sleep, and I wouldn't be surprised if Bennett is somewhere doing just that. And if you want to be alert for work tomorrow you should do the same. Goodnight, honey."

"Goodnight, Ted. I'm sorry I put you through this." Where was Bennett, she thought. If she waited until tomorrow to look further it might be too late. His business might be over and he might be gone. She had a week's worth of newspapers to toss, but fortunately hadn't. She sat on the carpet in the living room and stared at the stack of papers she'd dropped in front of her. Douglas Bennett's business was occurring at this very moment or was destined for the next day. First things first. Where was he now? He could be registered somewhere under another name. Well, Bennett was all she had to work with. She arranged the newspapers by date and started with the earliest one. Hotel Astor? No. That was where the mayor and all the stars in the universe had gone to the Equity Ball honoring Ruth Elder. Ted would have covered that one. She turned pages. Maybe the Stratford at 11th East 32nd Street, "appealing to a discerning clientele." Lily telephoned. He wasn't there. Oh, maybe 14 East 60th Street, "a hotel residence in the heart of the Social Center at the Plaza Entrance to Central Park." Not in residence. Her hands were tired of flipping pages, her finger hurt from dialing and her back was aching. The last newspaper. She opened it and wearily turned the pages. Brothels? Not if he had business to conduct the next day, and Mr. Sly and Moody didn't strike her as the brothel type. Maybe Ted was right about the park bench. Either that or Douglas Bennett simply wasn't in New York City. She was about to close the newspaper when --- "Wait!"

HOTEL GRAMATAN

Bronxville, N.Y.

A QUIET HOME-LIKE HOTEL

Directly at Station train service

Half hour electric Tel 3150

Lily's tired fingers dialed. "Has Mr. Douglas Bennett arrived yet?" She tapped her fingers on the table. "Thank you so much. No, not at this time. I'll wait until morning." Yes!! She raised both hands in triumph, then dialed Tenisha's number, the time be damned.

♦ ♦ ♦

Lily and Tenisha decided that Hotel Gramatan was out of their league. Another call about the cost of a stay there made that clear. There was no time to waste. This was a matter for the police. A call to Inspector Kirk yielded an underling; the inspector was not at work at eleven o'clock at night. A tenacious Lily refused to be turned off by the desk sergeant. She insisted on the inspector's home telephone number. The desk sergeant would not oblige. Lily hunkered down for a long night of telephone calls, which got to the point of the sergeant hanging up when he heard her voice. Too bad her uncle was not on duty tonight, she thought, although the results may have been worse. He would have lectured her before he hung up. Eventually, she wore the sergeant down. She was monopolizing the line and preventing serious callers from getting through, so although the desk sergeant refused to give her the inspector's number, he did dial it for her and make the connection. The inspector was not pleased.

"Do you realize it's past eleven? I don't model for a living, I do real work --- for eight, ten, twelve hours a day. What do you want and why do you want it now?"

"I'm so sorry to disturb you, Inspector Kirk, but there's an important development in the Lizette Frere case. Douglas Bennett has returned to New York with blackmail in mind, and it's related to Lizette Frere's murder. He's not the caring, hardworking father you believe him to be, unless you mean caring and hardworking on his own behalf. I'll tell you all I know when I see you, Inspector, but you must follow him and find out exactly what his business is here on this trip. He's staying at Hotel Gramatan in Bronxville. I'm not saying he's a murderer, but he knows more about the murder than he's told you. He may not stay at the hotel long. Please, Inspector, send your men undercover to track his activities. I won't deny you your sleep; I know you work hard. You can join them in the morning."

"Miss Chasen, I say this respectfully: You are a nut job! You pull Douglas Bennett out of left field to front and center of a murder case with no justification for doing so."

"I said I'd tell you ---"

"And you want my men to invade another jurisdiction and me to go running to Bronxville because your imagination has been fed by some of those ridiculous clothes you model and too many mystery novels. Stay out of police business. We're well on the way to solving the case, and we don't need --- no, I'll say it -- we resent your amateur interference. Now hang up your receiver or I'll be forced to be impolite and hang up mine."

Lily held the receiver, stunned, and heard the click. She dialed Tenisha. "The inspector hung up on me. Whatever Bennett intends to do he'll do without detection."

"Margaret gets in at 7 A.M. I hate to lie, so I'll call and say that a serious family matter makes it impossible for me to show up for work today."

"That's not a lie?"

"No. It is a serious family matter, it's just not my family."

"I'll call Bernie and tell him a situation beyond my control makes it impossible for me to model today."

"What situation beyond your control?"

"The police refusal to get on Bennett's tail. I can't force them to."

"What other information did the hotel give you when you called?"

"Besides the exorbitant charges? That breakfast is at 8:30."

"I'll meet you at the information booth at Grand Central Terminal at 7:45, and we'll catch the eight o'clock train. We can manage on seven hours sleep. No stylish clothes, please. We don't want to stand out. I may stand out, but I'll see what I can do. The Gramatan is a rather White hotel. See you in the morning."

CHAPTER TWENTY-FIVE

Grand Central Terminal always filled Lily with awe. The cavernous space, the vaulted, seemingly mile-high windows, the ornate stonework and the people, like miniatures when seen from the top of the sweeping staircases on either end. Ticket windows flanked one side and track entries the other, with the circular information center in mid floor, grounding the gorgeous setting that would otherwise probably fly away. Oh, what she could do with an apartment the size and grandeur of Grand Central! The thought was never out of her head whenever she appeared to catch a train to somewhere. She and Tenisha arrived at almost the same time. There were scatterings of people on the terminal floor, but only minutes later, after they had purchased their round-trip tickets to Bronxville, hundreds of people had appeared, seemingly from nowhere, on their way to or from train tracks or lined by the dozen in front of ticket windows. The morning rush hour had begun. The women walked silently to Track 15. Suddenly Tenisha put an arm on Lily's shoulder and pointed ahead. They slowed their pace. There was a woman in a stylish coat and hat. The coat looked like the one Ruth Elder had worn in an ad for La Belle Femme. The hat was the popular Patou felt, and an obvious original. Lily smiled, but Tenisha stared relentlessly ahead. She had recognized the back of the woman and her walk. As the woman turned aside to allow a mother and two children to pass through the track entrance before her, Lily's smile faded. Clearly profiled, not a dozen feet before them, was Sheila Wainwright Davenport.

"She'll think we're trailing her."

"We won't get in the same car, Ten. We'll get in the car after hers. Rats, she got in the last car."

They hurried past as she entered and moved to the next car up. They looked through the glass of the door connecting their cars. Sheila Davenport sat, her left profile clearly visible, her hands in her lap.

"Should one of us follow her?"

"Where --- to the beauty salon, her tailor, the Botanical Garden? Today's worry is what Douglas Bennett is up to. Coincidences do happen; so, she's on the same train, so what? I'd feel more secure if two of us were checking on Bennett. We'll make a note of what stop she gets off at, Ten, and let it go at that."

At each stop they jumped to their feet to look through the glass of the connecting door. Tired of this, they began to take turns. Ten minutes, twenty minutes, twenty-five minutes.

"She's joining Bennett in Bronxville, Ten."

They allowed Mrs. Davenport to exit first, then they quickly followed, pulling their coat collars high to cover half their faces. Across the wide expanse of road stood a majestic multi-level vision of creamy stucco walls, red tile roofs and graceful arches and gables. They seemed to be hanging from a hillside, and as they drew near, they saw the hotel's street-level shops and the elegant dome that marked the entrance to HOTEL GRAMATAN. They entered, keeping well behind Mrs. Davenport. She stopped at the desk, and a clerk with clarifying gestures pointed the way. Lily and Tenisha approached the desk clerk and asked for Mr. Bennett. Were they expected? They were. They were not listed as expected.

Ah, but they were with Mrs. Davenport, a bit delayed in greeting a guest they knew. What guest? Lily had noted several social headliners, and pulled Mrs. Hess's name out of the society pages hat. They were directed to one of the parlors. As they approached it, they shrank back and turned sideways, as Bennett and Davenport exited, talking about the greenery and the brisk air. A quick look inside revealed a room clothed in turn-of-the-century comfort with at least a dozen people laughing and chatting. They followed the couple through a number of arched porches before they stopped at one relatively unoccupied, pulled two chairs side-by side facing the shrubbery beyond, and turned toward each other. From a distance of twenty feet, it was impossible to hear what they were saying, but the women noted the expressions on their faces as they talked. At the outset, Bennett did all the talking. Mrs. Davenport's expression changed from acquiescent to surprised to alarmed and to quiet. Bennett was apparently allowing his words to penetrate deeply, because he did not speak for several minutes. He must then have asked her a question, because her response was easily read: "No." She vigorously shook her head, re-crossed her legs away from her companion and clasped her hands as a young lady would in a schoolroom. The young detectives turned to each other from time to time in mock conversation, but the objects of their observation were too engrossed to notice. After what seemed like hours, but Ten's watch revealed was only fifteen minutes, the couple rose and moved on. They stopped in front of the card room. Mrs. Davenport declined to enter. Mr. Bennett said something to her, entered the room and joined a game that was about to begin. Mrs. Davenport wandered the premises. She looked in on parlors, sitting rooms, writing rooms, the ballroom, without seeming to see any of them, bumping often into other guests even in uncrowded corridors. Although she was dressed for the outdoors, she seemed not to be aware of the warm interior. Tenisha and Lily were about to collapse from heat prostration. When Mrs. Davenport returned to the front desk, they both plopped, twenty feet behind, into lobby chairs. The desk clerk waved to them and called Mrs. Davenport's attention to them. She turned an impassive gaze at the two women and walked toward them. They sat up straight, then rose to their feet. She stood before them, staring, and didn't utter a word.

"We're here to help you, Mrs. Davenport," said Tenisha. "It wasn't our purpose in coming here, but since you've spoken to Mr. Bennett it is our purpose now."

"Are you in Mr. Bennett's employ?"

"Heavens, no! Perhaps we can sit somewhere and talk. I didn't notice anyone in the writing room as we passed it."

Mrs. Davenport remained silent, but followed the women. Several writing tables lined the walls of the room, and the young women pulled up two additional chairs around one of the desks.

"We weren't following you, Mrs. Davenport. We came here to see what Mr. Bennett was up to, and apparently it was to meet with you. Since you're so adept at having people followed, it doesn't seem fair for you to be angry at us for following people to get information that will lead to the arrest of the murderer of Lizette Frere. She was a colleague and a friend."

"I hope that your following people has yielded more information. than mine has. What have I, my husband and Mr. Bennett got to do with the death of Lizette Frere, Miss Chasen?"

"We haven't determined that yet, but if you will help us achieve our purpose, we will try to help you achieve yours."

"You know my purpose?"

"To determine whether your husband had an affair with Miss Frere, whether he did or not if your marriage is salvageable, and whether you want it salvaged. And Douglas Bennett has given information to you and asked questions of you that make you wonder whether you've been "taken," as an heiress and as a wife."

"The time for evasion and subterfuge is past, Miss Chasen. I realize that now. My husband does not realize that, and sends his father to say the words he cannot, dare not say. I have been lied to, and the assumption has been that I would be too embarrassed. to fight back. Embarrassed I will be when my husband's behavior becomes public, but not THAT embarrassed. My father's spirit has always risen up in me at every challenge and I will not be made a fool of any longer or pretend my marriage is what it is not. What can you say to me that I do not already know?"

"Your husband did not send his father to you. We can assure you of that. In fact, he insisted that his father do no such thing."

"But you think my husband may have murdered Miss Frere."

"Or you."

"That would be rather extreme action to take to avoid embarrassment."

Lily smiled as Sheila Davenport echoed her earlier thought, but Tenisha replied quietly to the heiress, "Having your husband followed for two years may be regarded as extreme action. Mr. Bennett wants you to keep La Belle Femme afloat. Will you, do it?"

"Without my check, Miss Jones, that company will be unable to fill and deliver its orders. I'm needed, not as I would like to be, but needed nonetheless."

"Your husband could always borrow from Wainwright Travel without your knowledge, if he's desperate."

"He cannot. I check the books monthly. He can only use his salary, which is generous, but hardly sufficient to meet the needs of his growing enterprise."

"Are you going to lend him the money?"

"I might. I am a businesswoman, as well as a wife, and I intend to continue as a businesswoman, whether I continue as a wife or not."

"Did you really think your husband was interested in Lizette Frere?"

"I wasn't sure, Miss Chasen; I'm still not sure."

"But your business sense may predominate, and you may invest in his company anyway."

"I may want a piece of the company. Mr. Bennett is pushing me for a decision, but I can think quickly. Do you both intend to continue following me?"

"Yes, we will. Do you mind?"

"Not at all, Miss Chasen. I know I'm innocent, but I hesitate to trust either Mr. Bennett or my husband. I'll feel more secure knowing that two women, more aware of the facts than the police, are watching over me. I'm not the kind of woman who shrieks or falls to pieces when trouble arises, so you'll have to be perceptive to the actual state of things if circumstances turn deadly. And now, if you'll excuse me, I must book accommodations for the night and telephone my personal maid to come with ensembles suitable for the evening and morning hours. My business with Mr. Bennett should be done by then." She nodded her goodbye.

"Well, we can't stay here. We have to be at work tomorrow."

"How can we leave now, Ten? She may be in danger—or a consummate liar, and if so, Douglas Bennett, offensive though he is, may be in danger."

"Then I say we aim to leave for work tomorrow morning by the eight o'clock train. If unfinished business forces us to catch the ten o'clock train, we'll have almost half an hour to dream up a reasonable excuse."

"I'm not sure I have enough in my checking account to pay for an evening here, Ten. Do you?"

"No, but by the time the check turns sour we'll have next week's salary to use. Bread and crackers for a week won't kill either one of us."

They walked with determination to the reservation desk and requested a small room. The desk clerk they had spoken to earlier had been replaced by another. The current clerk examined Lily's check. She examined Tenisha's check. She reached for the telephone and dialed. "Yes sir, Chasen, Lily Ann Chasen and Tenisha Jones, sharing a room. Is there someone staying here who can vouch for you?" she asked above the mouthpiece.

"Mrs. Sheila Davenport," Lily said smoothly.

The clerk repeated this, listened to the response, and hung up the receiver. "Please return in half an hour and we'll let you know if we can accommodate you."

The two women explored the hotel for twenty minutes, noting that Mr. Bennett was still in the card room. As they approached the lobby they saw Mrs. Davenport hailed as she passed the desk and spoken to briefly before she moved on.

The desk clerk smiled and produced one key for each and a card. The key read "Room 113." The card read "Lily Ann Chasen and Tenisha Jones, Honored Guests, Hotel Gramatan. Checks accepted for shops and restaurant and room charges."

"If they go to their rooms we can dress for the evening. Otherwise, we shouldn't have them out of sight."

"I agree, Lee, but dressing for the evening will be an exercise in creativity; all we have is what we're wearing. I'm willing to blow a few dollars on a scarf or shawl in one of the shops here, as soon as we feel we can spare five minutes from our quarries."

"Sounds like a plan to me. I'm starved, and it looks like the Davenport/Bennett combo, are too. Diners beware! A nefarious pair is en route to dine!"

Ten and Lily boldly sat at a table facing the pair in the elegant, old-world dining room. Bennett had never met either of them personally, though a description from his son could not be ruled out. Sheila Davenport would be relieved they were there, unless that was what she wanted them to think. Douglas Bennett had just placed a hand-printed sheet on the empty plate in front of his table-mate as well as on his own. They had pens in hand, and were apparently discussing the paper's contents line by line. Words were added and deleted. They were so absorbed that they didn't notice the fruit salads placed before them or the glasses being filled with water as they spoke. Ten and Lily looked at each other. The deal was in progress.

"Someone's missing," said Tenisha. Lily nodded. "Since this investigative jaunt is costing us plenty, let's get all we can out of it. Shall you call or I?"

"I'll call. Don't let them take my salad."

For the sake of realism, Tenisha gave occasional attention to her salad, but she was focused on the changing dynamics at the nearby table. When Lily returned, she saw that Sheila Davenport was now composed and serene and Douglas Bennett was now agitated.

"He may not want her as partner, high stakeholder or whatever it is she's demanding."

"She might cut into the cream he's getting Lee, and his dislike of the fashion business may not be as acute as his dislike of a woman in charge, to any degree. When will junior arrive?"

"In forty minutes, if he catches the next train. I heard 'I thought so' in his voice. He said to make sure that nothing is signed."

"As if we could stop it! But why is it necessary? Even if his wife signs an agreement, it isn't valid without his signature on it. His father can't sign for him."

"Legally, no, but like his father or not, he may not want him jailed for forgery. If he were willing to allow that, he wouldn't be augmenting his income to win his silence. What page are they on?"

"Their fourth. Look, she's signing. He sure looks grim. I wonder what she's saying."

Sheila Davenport rose and began walking to the exit. Halfway there she turned toward Bennett, who was hastily signing for the bill. She continued walking as he scrambled after her.

"She's sticking him with the bill!"

As she passed their table, with Bennett in pursuit, she spoke as if to the air, "I'm on board if George agrees."

"He'll agree," softly chorused Lee and Ten, as they signaled for their bill. What other choice did her husband have? Mrs. Davenport reached the lobby before Mr. Bennett. She lifted a flyer from a table filled with sheets detailing the hotel's activities.

"Here at eight o'clock," they heard her say, before she walked toward the elevator. Bennett did not look happy. He waited for the desk clerk to be free. "Room, another night." He was being forced to stay longer. As he sullenly walked off, they hastened to the table for a flyer before following him. The flyer read, "Bronxville Library Ball, 8-11 P.M., Hotel Gramatan." The word TONIGHT formed a diagonal banner on the upper left. The charge was $30, pricey for an auto mechanic of any caliber.

"I'll bet she's making him pay," said Tenisha. "The revenge of a woman thwarted!"

Lily had kept her eyes on the elevator. The numbers above it indicated it had stopped at all floors. Presumably Mrs. Davenport had gone to her room, though it seemed too early to dress for the evening. "I'll check this out, Ten. Follow Bennett."

Douglas Bennett wandered the hotel, seemingly in a daze, much like Sheila Davenport had done earlier, when her father-in-law had sprung shocking news on her. He finally went to the shops on the entrance level, and Tenisha wandered there with him. He fingered neckties, shirts, wallets and sundry male items before turning to the children's shop. Outside elaborate doll houses stood many a horse and buggy alongside Model T's and Hupmobiles. Miniature furniture and house occupants were in the rooms and at the entrance doors. Bennett looked at them briefly before moving on to toys for boys: cowboys and WWI soldier figures, sturdy wooden wagons, building blocks, guns, bows and arrows, chemistry and magic sets. Tenisha wondered, was there a child he sought to please? He had no grandchildren. Was he intent on gifting a youngster he knew or had befriended? The store was getting crowded. She didn't want to get too close to him, but she didn't want to lose him either. Over many heads she saw that he was having something wrapped. He presented his "Honored Guest" card and left with the gaily wrapped package. She made her way to the counter, cut in front of a customer who was explaining the kind of gift she was looking for, and ignoring the outraged "Well!" from said customer asked the saleslady what the gentleman she had just served had purchased. It was a BB gun, "quite safe, with cotton pellets." Tenisha caught sight of Bennett as he entered the elevator. She waited for the next one and headed to her room, nearly crashing into Lily as she opened the door.

"George Davenport's here! I saw him crossing the street to the hotel."

They took the stairs two at a time, and reached the lobby as George Davenport entered. He heartily shook their hands. "Thank you for calling. My successes of late seem to be matched with impending disasters."

"Your father is in room 404, and your wife is in 223. Disaster relief is not available, but two sets of sympathetic ears are."

George Davenport smiled wryly. "You certainly get my drift," he said, and he walked off.

"He's not going to their rooms!"

"With poison in the air, Lee, a private dressing down could prove dangerous to all parties. A public dressing down and apology is more likely to be civil -- and safer."

They sat in the lobby, watched the passing crowd and waited. Fifteen minutes later the elevator door opened to reveal the adversaries. Lee and Ten ducked behind a potted palm. From between the leaves, they saw George Davenport stop briefly at the desk and receive a word and gesture. The two women followed them as they made a winding way around the first floor, stopping at a sitting room. Davenport ushered the other two in. The sign he looped around the door handle swung wildly as he shut the door. It said, "Do Not Disturb."

"How long will Sitting Room 3 be private?" asked Tenisha after they had returned to the lobby.

"We've allowed the party no more than an hour. You should be able to use it by six o'clock."

"Will they require any other special services this evening? I ask only because if they've made other plans they won't be able to join us for bridge at six o'clock."

"We've merely been alerted to type a contract for them when they conclude their meeting. That should not keep them from a game of bridge."

Lily and Tenisha walked through several outdoor, arcaded porch areas, before finding one sheltered from the early evening breeze and for which their sweaters were adequate. They rocked on the large chairs, thinking. At half past five the sign was still on the door, but at quarter to six it was gone. Ten suggested a stroll on three other floors. The light seeping out from under each of three doors indicated that the objects of their pursuit were in their rooms.

"This looks like a business evening for our trio. What can be gained by our staying?"

"You're right." Lily turned toward the elevator "We'd save a small bundle if we left now. It would be a nice evening for dancing if our men were here." They exited the elevator and walked down the corridor. "But hardly likely to help us solve a -- oh, my!"

A man was bending over a prostrate figure outside their room. He rose at the exclamation and rushed down the opposite corridor, pushing something deeply in a pocket of his over-sized coat as he ran. Ten and Lee reached the woman, who was lying on her back and moaning. She was bleeding from a deep cut on her chin, and the side of her forehead was turning purple. Lily hurried into the room to call for help. It arrived quickly, before the women could do more than raise the young woman's head and apply cold water to her wounds. "She'll be all right," the doctor said after a quick examination. "That was some fall." Two men lifted the injured housemaid onto a cot and carried her to the elevator, while a third picked up the towels, scattered around the corridor, that she had intended as replacements in the bathroom.

Tenisha looked around the floor, bent and picked up a rock. She looked above their door ledge. "Slim enough to fit there, and heavy enough to do damage. It would be foolish to leave just yet, don't you think, Lee?"

"A scarf and a shawl, now what can we do with these?" pondered Lily.

"Davenport wasn't wearing a humongous tweed coat when he arrived."

"They will definitely dress up plain blouses, but our blouses yell 'daytime' with a vengeance."

"We don't know what Bennett wore when he arrived. Sheila Davenport certainly wasn't wearing it. I was grateful for deep pockets when Ted pulled a crowbar out of his to threaten the man standing under the lamppost outside my building, but these deep pockets hold danger for us. We're in somebody's way."

"The skirts will do if we draw attention elsewhere."

"Lee, are you listening to me?"

"Yes, my blabber is meant to distract my pounding heart from the meaning of it all."

"You're a threat; that's a given, but eliminating you won't stop George Davenport's eyes from wandering."

"It's a start, but how could his wife arrange this so fast?"

"She's had plenty of detective practice the past two years, but her husband or his father may have wanted to put her mind at ease about you and, long-shot possibility, about me. Anyway, we can breathe for a while, since La Belle Femme will stay financially afloat; the liquidity problem seems to have been resolved."

"I want to breathe for more than a while, Ten. Even if we're muted threats in one area, we're a threat to one or more of them if we pursue Lizette's murderer."

"So, what are we wearing, Lee?"

Chapter Twenty-Six

Lily put the menu down. "If they served tuna salad for dinner, we could save a bundle. I'm asking for a Caesar Salad."

"It's not on the menu."

"I'm asking for it anyway."

The dining room was bustling with movement as entering guests, en route to their tables, maneuvered around seated ones. Table settings glittered under the chandeliers, and the clink of glassware and assorted voices made music. The Davenports appeared side by side, he allowing her to precede him, with Douglas Bennett bringing up the rear. Ten and Lee had reserved a table that would allow easy viewing of the trio, as well as allow for a hasty exit, should that be necessary. The trio's activities mirrored those of the duo at lunch. Each removed a set of papers from individual envelopes. This was obviously the final copy; no pens were visible. There was agitated finger-pointing by George Davenport, with minimal response from his wife and father. Lily shook her head.

"Sad. A contract is a contract, and this one was surely clear from the outset, but still Davenport argues and questions."

"Signed it against part of his will, it seems, the part that doesn't want to be constrained by or obligated to the woman aboard."

Lily nodded. "But the part of his will that wanted the funding won the argument."

Douglas Bennett seemed tolerant of both the anguish of his son and the serenity of his daughter-in-law. He put copies of the contract into their envelopes and left the dining room with them. Tenisha left the table and returned a short while later.

"He picked up a key to the hotel vault."

Bennett did not return, leaving his son and daughter-in-law eating a quiet dinner. Sporadic conversation was initiated by the wife with limited response. Tenisha and Lily waited until the Davenports left before leaving themselves. Fabulous sounds floated through the lobby. Someone was boldly striking out a jazz tune on the piano in the lounge. Festively attired folk were talking and swaying to faint rhythms that permeated the sitting rooms, and it seemed that only in the card room could one find two men, oblivious to the sounds, solemnly playing their hands. Tenisha and Lily followed the Davenports to the ballroom. The Bronxville Library Ball was already under way. The couple strolled to the bar for drinks. It was then that Lily and Tenisha fully saw Sheila Davenport that evening. They saw an elegant woman, relaxed, with a faint smile, whose hair, gown and shoes complemented a demeanor that turned heads. It was only after that effect had registered that they noticed her jewelry.

"She's stunning," said Lee.

The Davenports stood long at the bar, not drinking, just talking. Finally, George Davenport led his wife to the dance floor. They danced for a long time.

"They look right together, Lee. Is it my imagination, or is he holding her closer now?"

They looked around the room. The gay colors, swirling fabrics and cut crystal chandeliers relaxed them. Ten smiled.

"So, this is what's billed as a 'quiet, home-like hotel.' I wish my home were like this. Look, there's Bennett. When did he come in? We're slipping in this 'home-like' atmosphere." They moved within ten feet of him, each wishing she had a male escort to make her presence more reasonable.

Lily approached Bennett. "Such a wonderful institution. The Bronxville Library deserves all the funding it can get, don't you agree."

"Yes, of course. Excuse me."

A waiter rushing from clear across the ballroom, brushed past Bennett, who with a firm hand on his right shoulder stopped him, "What's the matter?"

"Some fool locked the spare liquor cabinet in the alcove. I need the manager to unlock it."

Bennett moved quickly toward the hotel photographer. He nodded toward his dancing son, encountering resistance from the photographer who pointed to several other couples, until a handshake produced acquiescence to his request.

Tenisha looked solemnly at Lily. "He's in an all-fired hurry." They quickened their pace to reach him as he moved toward the alcove, and the photographer stopped the dancing Davenports requesting their photograph. Facing the spot he indicated was the alcove sheltered by a palm tree. Bennett had disappeared behind the tree. As the photographer was about to emit the blinding flash, something circular poked through the leaves. Ten and Lee leaped at the tree, sending it and Bennett crashing to the floor as the missile took off, splintering the mirror behind the posing couple. George Davenport ran forward and stopped horrified as he saw his father.

"You don't need her anymore, George!" hurled the older man. George Davenport let fly with a right to the Bennett jaw that could be heard twenty feet away.

CHAPTER TWENTY-SEVEN

Tenisha Jones and Lily Ann Chasen looked around in wonder. The red and white tablecloths looked ready to sweep out from under the dishes and glasses as if by magic and join the dancers moving in hectic joy around the floor. A dapper, elegant gentleman left the piano, motioned a break to the orchestra and descended on them.

"Welcome to the Cotton Club!" Duke Ellington gripped their hands firmly and sat down. "A'Lelia said that if I wanted to meet you amazing ladies I'd have to get you in the Club. I laughed when I read that the good inspector said you were playing detective. You sure weren't playing! I hope that neither of you plays the piano; I wouldn't want my job here to be in jeopardy."

"I do play piano," said Lily, "but I'm the wrong color for entertaining here."

"And I'm the wrong color for guesting here!" exclaimed Tenisha.

They all laughed.

"Someday it will be different and some other crazy rule will be in place, maybe against exceptionally tall people or women who wear pale lipstick. Congratulations, congratulations on closing the case! You did astonishing work! Your aunt is ecstatic, Tenisha; she can't stop talking about it. She called to ask if the boys and I would play at a soiree in honor of you both, and a one-minute request turned into a half hour speech on all you both did and how proud she is of you. My end of the conversation consisted of one word --- yes. And it seems you've pulled off an equally great achievement, keeping the Davenport marriage intact. I heard from a friend that when they were in their Palm Beach home last weekend to get away from the more zealous newsmen and photographers in New York, a bee flew through the window as Sheila and George were having coffee, and she swatted the buzzing creature with the Coulet Couture funding contract. Then, exclaiming 'our commitment is not built on paper,' she crumpled the pages and tossed them into the fireplace."

"Business commitments certainly are built on paper," countered Tenisha.

"A fireplace in Florida in December?" questioned Lily.

"It's symbolism. The story is making the rounds. Symbolism is making the rounds. Personal shocks can make you reconsider what's truly important to you, often make you realign your priorities. Anyway, there's hope for that relationship, and that's a big something for which you ladies are responsible. Now I hope that you're both prepared to dance all night, because my boys are looking forward to taking turns sweeping you off your feet --- literally, the way some of them dance. Your exhaustion begins in five minutes, soon as they get back from their break." He put up two hands to ward off possible complaints and headed back to the piano.

"This is fabulous," gushed Tenisha, "but I did try to persuade auntie to let Ted and Donald join us. 'Women celebs only,' she said. 'They'll have their turn next time. ' "

"I hope she didn't mean after we solve another murder. Bernie told me that Sheila Davenport persuaded him to include adaptations of some Coulet Couture pieces in the charity showing you got him into --- he's happy about it, he's happy about it --- and she's decided that the adaptations should be preceded the month before by a showing of the complete Coulet collection. She said that his stunning, innovative designs would show Americans what was exciting the French. The adventurous might even opt for the originals. She was sure that a presentation like this would imprint the Coulet name in women's minds, and establish him as a design force in this country. When I heard this, I called her with a suggestion. I said that her black tie event should have floor-to-ceiling murals in black and white of people and places associated with Paris. They would make a striking backdrop to the Coulet line. I thought the centerpiece should be Josephine Baker, a link between two countries, an American who's the toast of Paris."

"What a great idea! It's about time that a Negro is front and center in New York. Did she agree?"

"Yes, she did, but I had another suggestion." Lily poured champagne into their glasses. "I thought that a match for the fabulous Miss Baker eight feet tall on the wall, should be a fabulous Negro model on the runway. Welcome to the club, Ten!"

Tenisha's eyes glowed, as she and Lily raised their glasses in a joyous clink. "Whoopie!" they screamed at the top of their lungs, but their shouts were swallowed up in the musical uproar the Duke's men had just begun.

The End

www.ingramcontent.com/pod-product-compliance
Lightning Source LLC
LaVergne TN
LVHW021821060526
838201LV00058B/3472